DOUBLE FEATURE
KILLER BURGERS
Welcomes you to:
Gourmets and Ghosts
cover art
w.p. Quigley
design
Madi Quinn w.p. Quigley
managing editors
John A. McColley S.N. Humphreys
contributing writers
Madi Quinn
John A. McColley w.p. Quigley
director of programming
w.p. Quigley
ASCENDENT
© 2023 Ascendent Publishing
All rights reserved.
www.ascendentpublishing.com
AF483819

Tonight's Menu:

Tonight's Menu:
$2

DOUBLE FEATURE
Year 2 Preview
$30

A Word from
the
Projectionist
$3

amuse bouche
"Shift Change"
sous chef John A. McColley
$34

apertif
"Tootsie Pop"
sous chef w.p. Quigley
$5

Plat principal
"Chef de
Cuisine"
Head Chef Madi Quinn
$37

entree
"The Unbeating
Heart"
Head Chef Madi Quinn
$10

DESSERT & COFFEE
Closing Credits
$58

A WORD FROM THE PROJECTIONIST:

My my my, where does the time go? It was just over a year ago when all of this nonsense kicked off – DOUBLE FEATURE magazine, ASCENDENT Publishing, when there was a moment I stopped and asked myself a couple of pertinent questions before I committed myself to trying to make all of it work.

why am I doing this?

The concept of DOUBLE FEATURE magazine started as an off-hand remark a close friend of mine made towards the end of the first "appearance" I made as a bonafide author at an event called the Plymouth Punk Rock Market, here in the good 'ol Commonwealth of Massachusetts. My novel that wasn't due to come out until July was almost a year away from publication at the time, and she'd basically suggested that I just sorta put something out in the meantime to keep me and my name on the minds of the people who'd bought my crazy-ass anthology, *ChaoS/HeaveN*.

I didn't put a lot of thought into it, and decided it would just be two long-ish short short stories that together would be equivalent to a novella in length and I'd call it double feature.

From there, I mentioned the idea to another friend of mine, who is no longer my friend (story for another time), who made the suggestion that it could be a semi-regular thing that I do in between books. The word magazine got dropped, and well, I don't think I need to bore you with anymore of the details.

But why, though, Wally?

The act of writing, as in physical setting down of words to paper, is easy. The continued practice of writing, completing short stories and novellas and novels and the like is hard. I've been writing shit my whole life; I didn't actually complete a first draft of any novel I've ever started until I was forty-six. *ChaoS/HeaveN* was supposeed to come after *The Ascendant* – my petty, childish, narcississtic older sisters did their thing and *CH* came out first. But just getting something completed and published and out into the fucking world was nothing short of a lifelong nightmare for me.

I didn't want anybody else to have to deal with that who didn't have to, and so DOUBLE FEATURE adopted the concept of the two "shorts" at the beginning to try and get some real face time for creative people I knew who were fantastic people and had a voice that needed to be heard (read). Getting past that first hurdle is pretty fucking tough. I felt like if I made it that much easier for someone else, I'd be doing my part for the art form as a whole.

The second part of the answer to that question came from my own personal experience in self-publishing with Amazon KDP, insofar as that particular chapter of my writing/publishing career could be a summarized as nothing short of a full-on Faustian bargain that ended with me already embittered and soured on the entire industry.

Amazon KDP, and the Kindle device has destroyed the written word as both an art form and a viable means to fashion out a career or means of living. Rather than boring you with the details of why this is a sad, sobering fact of writing as industry and an art form, if you be an author, poet, publisher, agent, or what have you – I urge you, dear reader, to first do some extra reading and take a deep dive into the disheartening negative consequences that have become a reality as a direct result of Amazon's KDP program, the Kindle device & Amazon's policies regarding publishing on the Kindle, and –hey, why not- Amazon's general business practices.

The time doth approacheth when Amazon won't just dominate 87% percent of the market – that time is already here – it will dominate 99% of it and then well, shit we might as all just stop writing altogether and let AI writers do all the thinking, feeling, and responding for us.

But, until that time, I felt the imprimatur to try to steer as many new, hopeful authors and writers away from having to go through that experience firsthand themselves and become as prematurely embittered as I had. Writing and publishing a book had been a dream of mine since I was child; to experience that loss of control over one's own art, to be basically dry-fucked out of the financial rewards (however much of a pittance it was, it was still *mine*, goddamnit), and then to realize that the only copies you were ever going to sell via Amazon were the ones that they as a company were willing to market you up for – which meant how dirt cheap/low of a price you're willing to go.

There are far, far too many really great authors selling their work for 99 cents right now on that literary hellscape and I am absolutely not exaggerating when I say that it breaks my heart.

DOUBLE FEATURE, in the year that it has existed as a literary and periodical entity, has probably only barely skated across a thousand copies sold; we're obviously a niche magazine with some....extreme content to say the least.

But the opportunity I – and we – have tried to present to authors and writers is that unique chance and platform to express themselves without that nagging, overriding sense of having to reign themselves in for the sake of selling an extra copy or two. Fuck that hot sauce, as it were. In that regard, DOUBLE FEATURE is as honest and pure a periodical you'll find floating around out there.

From our very first short, "Amanda", way back in December of last year, that sincerity of spirit and creativity had quite literally been under attack. It's a story I don't like to share, but I ended a twenty-three year friendship over that story (not with the author, with a person who had awful shit to say about it) because it became crystal clear to me that person wasn't interested in hearing new and fresh voices, he only wanted to hear and give merit to the ones that sounded most like his own.

Fuck that hot sauce, once again.

DOUBLE FEATURE #4, then, I am MOST proud to say, showcases the voice of my good friend and colleague Madi Quinn, whose voice absolutely is unlike my own in nearly every regard. Her tales *The Unbeating Heart* and *Chef de Cuisine* await you, but first – my own sort of tribute to her unique style...*Tootsie Roll.*

Because whatever it is I think I read....

-w.p. Quigley
November 2023

Tootsie Pop

w.p. Quigley

As I awake, a single television set turns on at my stirring. Displayed on the monitor is a simplistic animation; a boy approaches a cow from the left in a medium shot. The boy holds up what appears to be a lollipop.

"Mr. Cow,"

"Eeeeeyeeeees?"

"How many licks does it take to get to the Tootsie Roll center of a Tootsie Pop?"

"Eh, I don't know! I always end up biting. Ask Mr. Fox – he's much cleverer than I."

The television stops playing at this point, not finishing the commercial for whatever reason. I'm sure I'm about to find out.

Several overhead spotlights turn on the moment the television goes dark, as if to call immediate attention to my current situation. I am bound by my feet and chest to a chair in the center of an otherwise empty room. In front of me is a wall of televisions, each look as if they've been hooked into the same closed circuit. A single cable emerges from the small, black box positioned on the top of each television, and each of these cables reduces via splitters down to a single cable that presumably leads to its source transmitter.

This is the cast and crew's idea of stupid, elaborate prank it appears. We wrapped production on "Hammer and Nail 7: The Final Chapter" last night. They'd all hoped for a post-wrap celebration, even scheduled the time and place to meet-up. Of course, they had to cancel as the final shot we filmed was also the final shot in the movie, and it had to be perfect. Their minds were all on the party, and no matter how simple I made my instruction neither the actors, cameramen, support crew, *nobody* could follow the simple instructions I'd asked of them. We finally got a workable version of the shot after forty-six takes. Acceptable, not perfect, but at last I just was too frustrated and I let them go. They'll all thank me in the end.

"Folks, look. I know you're upset about last night. I would be too – but it's not something to hold a grudge about. So, joke's ov–"

The television comes on again, this time it displays one of the many hit pieces from countless movie critics on the *Hammer and Nail* series of horror movies I've had the privelege of writing and directing three entries therein, including the final two chapters.

"One would think that we'd seen the last of the 'torture porn' subgenre of horror films, especially given the level of misogyny and violence towards women characteristic of these films. Not so, as IT CAME FROM THE 617 Studios has just announced '*Hammer and Nail 7: The Final Chapter*' slated for release this summer. This loathsome entry will once again be helmed by controversial director j.p. Lamond who–"

The television cuts out to static, then back to off entirely.

I hear a door open behind me, then close. I hear footsteps, and then in front of me appears, clothed in brown robes with matching hood and face covering, a single figure. The hands are covered with similarly colored latex gloves, double gloved. I cannot tell if it is female or male hands as such; but then again, I likely shouldn't think of them as gendered as even that categorization is ignorant, backwards thinking these days. Maybe this is the point of this whole charade.

The individual produces a single sewing needle from underneath a sleeve. They hold it up, along with the index finger on the hand not holding the needle as if to say 'one'. The individual sticks the needle into my cheek without further ceremony.

"MOTHERFUCKER! How...how dare you?!?" I turn my attention away from my assailant and shout upwards at the microphone/loudspeaker I presume is somewhere in the room above and behind me.

"All of you, listen." I firm up my diaphragm and deliver an ultimatum.

"WE CAN LET THIS GO, RIGHT NOW, IF SOMEONE COMES IN AND UNTIES ME!"

The figure leaves the room.

A short time afterwards, another figure enters. The ritual is the same, except for where the person stabs me with their sewing needle. The second person puts theirs into the webbing between the pinky and ring finger on my left hand, which is tied behind my back.

"OH, I GET IT," I announce, once I've swallowed back my cry of pain. This isn't my cast and crew at all. This is some protest group making an ill-advised statement against the movies I direct. Somehow I knew my team wouldn't be responsible for a sick stunt like this.

"You're protesting 'TORTURE PORN' movies. I get it. And 'Tootsie Pop'...'torture porn'...nice touch. What happens when—"

The third individual enters as the second leaves. I can tell this because the door opens and closes but once.

The third needle is inserted into my right ear, piercing the eardrum, and spinning me on a psychotic merry-go-round of vertigo, nausea, and biting, reverberating pain. I am unable to respond, or even speak as I feel a single, warm trickle of blood run down the side of my face and down my neck.

I do not regain the ability to speak for what I believe to be anywhere from twenty to twenty-five more needles. It is the location of the last in this series that brings my capacity for verbal communication back to fore.

It is stuck directly into the urethra at the tip of my penis.

"Oh please god, please stop....I'm sorry! For whatever it is I've done, I'm sorry. *I'M SORRRY!*"

The television comes on again when my screamed apology concludes and the room falls silent. It is the second part of the Tootsie Pop commercial.

"Mr. Fox, how many licks does it take to get to the Tootsie Roll center of a Tootsie Pop?"

Mr. Fox, wearing sunglasses and speaking as if possessed by the spirit of Peter Lorre, responds:

"Why don't you ask Mr. Turrtle, he's been around for a lot longer than I. Me? I biiite."

The television snaps off again, and frantically I attempt to puzzle out what has been determined to be the "center of the Tootsie Pop" that whomever is doing this to me has settled upon. The needles keep coming, however, and achieving sustained, coherent thought is impossible...

...especially as I lose the ability to hold urine within my bladder and am forced to urinate. The piss still comes, albeit in pressurized droplets that force their way out from the needle stuck into the tip of my cock. I close my eyes as a universe of agony unfolds; stars of suffering fly past planets of raw pain while moons of misery orbit. And yet I still feel the needles going in – my feet, my hands, my face, my stomach.

I have lost count by the time I have forced all of the liquid waste from my bladder. And as if on cue, it is also the exact moment when I evacuate my bowels onto the chair I sit upon.

"I'll…I'll never…I'll never make…another…torture…tortureporn torcherpurn mooovy….a….gan," I manage to sputter out.

The television clicks on again.

"…amidst regular accounts that writer and director j.p. Lamond had not only sexually harassed several female members of the cast and crew, but even had even according to one account assaulted and raped 'Hammer and Nail 6' lead actress Shireen Thirlby. The allegations never resulted in any legal troubles for Lamond, although speculation continues…"

So that's who's responsible. No protestors, no film crew, just one bitch with a chip on her shoulder over one drunken night on set.

Shireen started telling anyone and everyone who'd listen about that night – *our night* – only after 'Hammer and Nail 6' became the first big box office draw after COVID had laid waste to the entire movie industry. She saw a second opportunity, on top of the one *I gave her* to capitalize and didn't hesitate, the proverbial fucking wolf in sheep's–

A needle is inserted into my right eye, noiselessly popping it, rendering it useless and me blind on that side. I am losing my hold…

WHATEVER IT IS I THINK I SEE BECOMES A TOOTSIE ROLL TO ME!

I look down with my good eye, and I see hundreds upon hundreds of Tootsie Rolls *(needles, j.p., they're needles not Tootsie Rolls)* sticking out of me. I am a Tootsie Roll. This is all far, far too funny for words. I begin to laugh, laugh uncontrollably as the Tootsie Rolls come in and stick Tootsie Rolls into my gums and tongue and teeth and lips. They stick Tootsie Rolls into my Tootsie Rolls and then Tootsie Rolls into my Tootsie Rolls.

Everything's Tootsie. Roll's I think I see.

There must be thousands of Tootsie Rolls. I am a candy store of red and brown and piss and blood leaking down.

The television comes on a final time. It seems the lad is exasperated! I am too. Maybe Mr. Turtle has an answer for us both.

"Mr. Turtle, how many licks does it take to get to the Tootsie Roll center of a Tootsie Pop?"

Mr. Turtle responds with the voice of elderly, senile old man. He's not gonna fucking know.

"I never made it without biting...ask Mr. Owl, for he is the wisest of us all."

No shit, kid. Why didn't you ask Mr. Owl first before fucking around with all these assholes? Mr. Cast and Crew wait no – Mr. Cow was his name. He didn't know. Mr. Torture Porn – no, why do I keep doing that – Mr. Fox. He was fucking useless. Then Mr. Sexual Assault. *DAMMIT!* Mr. Turtle. Nothing there.

I'm hungry. So hungry. Good thing I have Tootsie Rolls in my mouth to snack on. I bite down and taste their gooey gooey gummy goodness. Delicious.

"Mr. Owl, how many licks does it take to get to the Tootsie Roll center of a Tootsie Pop?"

"A good question. Let's find out. A – one...a – toohoo...three."

The owl bites down, and hands the now eaten lollipop back to the heartbroken and disappointed child.

"Three."

Three? This cannot be. I look down, and my chest, legs, stomach, and the parts of my face I can see are covered in sewing needles. The shirt and pants I am wearing are covered in blood. My entire body is on fire. The room begins to spin in and out of darkness. It was because I bit down! I shouldn't have taken a bite. We'll have to start over. The next figure to come in appears, and I mouth to him as such:

"Please...we have to start over. I bit down! Start over!"

The Tootsie Roll tilts its head to the side, and seems to agree. The Tootsie Roll inserts a Tootsie Roll into a nostril, and holds up the index finger of the hand not holding the needle. Oh thank God. We'll be able to get to the bottom of this soon enough.

The figures keep coming, and so does the candy.

(NOT CANDY. NEEDLES.)

Shut up, j.p.!

And then gleefully I begin to sing:

WHATEVER IT IS I THINK I SEE, BECOMES A TOOTSIE ROLL TO ME!!!

The UNBEATING Heart

The Unbeating Heart
Madi Quinn

The night closed its fingers around the decrepit building, cloaking everything in a thick coat of shadow. What had looked perfectly ordinary took on a sinister aspect in the fresh darkness, and deep in the middle of it was Josh Connors, looking lost and frightened once again.

Josh was an amateur ghost hunter, though he preferred the title "paranormal investigator," and his methods were just as amateur as his status. Josh's major problem in this respect was that he was utterly terrified of the dark, even at the age of nineteen. Still, even with the phobia, Josh had been obsessed with the supernatural since he was a very young child, wanting desperately to prove that there were real monsters under the bed and in the closet. He never found the merest scrap of evidence, no matter how clever his plan. His prey always eluded him, and he was made to look foolish.

He was feeling just as foolish now, in this rank basement reeking of mildew and coated with a thick layer of dust. Howard's tip that the old house on Osborn, long abandoned and with a history of violence, would be a sure-fire win was a bust. There was no activity at all in the dilapidated structure, and once more, Josh felt like a complete idiot.

He packed in the equipment he had, which was admittedly meager, consisting of three old cell phones, a flashlight, and his "spirit box", which was essentially a radio that tracked all up and down the band looking for signals. Though he'd paid a large amount of money for the spirit box, it hadn't yielded a thing. He was despondent; it was another wasted day. A Monday, no less; a reminder of how much money Josh didn't have.

The path he'd chosen wasn't always the road he'd walked. It was only a couple of years prior to Josh's ghost adventures that he'd been like any other average teenager. He'd studied for the most part, though he was not an honor roll student. He'd dated a girl named Melissa, someone that was very good for him. They'd made plans for going to college together, getting a home together, and even marriage and/or children. Melissa and Josh were inseparable; at least, they were until a horrible car accident ended up killing Melissa when a drunk driver plowed his car into the passenger side of Josh's Escort. Melissa died straight away, but the man who killed her walked away with minor injuries. He would, in time, be arrested and convicted of the incident, but there just was no closure for Josh.

Josh became obsessed with the idea of life after death, and even more obsessed with the notion of somehow contacting Melissa. He watched all the paranormal television programs and learned what he needed to know (or what he *thought* he needed to know) about being a paranormal investigator. He took his equipment and set out to find a ghost.

Unfortunately, Josh never found anything but old, ramshackle buildings and angry animals. His resolve was iron, but his skill was…lacking. He tried, again and again, but to no avail; the dead just didn't seem to want to talk to him. He even went into the old Ashton house, the one place that was all but guaranteed to be haunted, but still found nothing.

He climbed back out the basement window that he'd used to enter. There was a storm coming, the kind that you can smell before it begins, and a light rain had already begun to fall.

"Fantastic," Josh muttered.

Josh trudged wearily back home, and collapsed upon his bed, his eyes fixed on the ceiling. The normal distractions, music and television, no longer appealed to him. All that mattered was finding Melissa and talking with her again. Nothing else was worth the effort or the time.

He ran over the possible haunted areas of the city in his mind again, just as he did every other time he failed. Cemeteries, old hospitals, run down houses; he'd been to them all and found nothing. There was simply nothing else to try that he hadn't already tried.

"Alright then," he mumbled to himself. "We start over, back at the beginning."

Irongate Cemetery, the oldest one in the city, had been his first investigation, and he'd discovered in that place that people find the idea of sitting in a graveyard in the middle of the night to be off-putting, and little else. Nevertheless, he resolved to return to Irongate, and perhaps try a different grave or mausoleum. Perhaps he was just too fixated on Melissa, and couldn't get past finding her.

No, he would just try again. Something had to work. It HAD too.

Josh closed his eyes and fell fast asleep, a single tear running down his cheek as he drifted off.

The next day came, and Josh returned to his job at the local grocery store. His shift was uneventful; all he could think about was returning to Irongate that night, and his impending triumph. The moment his shift ended, he clocked out, tore off his uniform shirt, threw on a Faith No More t-shirt and his jacket, and set out to Irongate. He arrived just as the sun set, giving him little time to find a suitable location for his investigation while he could still see the headstones unaided. After several minutes of searching, he found a stone from 1896, a woman named Anne Chambers.

Something drew his attention to that grave, though he could not put a finger on it. It was just a good feeling, a hunch, so he began to set up near Anne Chambers' headstone. He set his digital recorder, one that he'd bought for lectures and classes that he rarely attended those days, down on top of the headstone, and turned on the spirit box. He closed his eyes and took a deep breath, and then began.

"Is there anyone here? I'm looking for Anne Chambers. If Anne is present here, please make yourself known. I have a recorder that can capture what you want to say, and this device in my hand lets us talk as well.

Silence. Even the crickets were quiet. Josh grimaced at what was already looking to be a potential failure.

"Anne Chambers? Please speak to me."

No response. The lights on his EM field meter

were still off, and nothing was coming through any of the other devices. It was, as always, a complete failure, and Josh felt his heart sink. He'd felt good about this one, as if…

"…yes…"

Clear as day, a voice, a woman's voice, spoke through the spirit box. Josh turned sharply to the small device that he'd set near the headstone, his mouth agape in disbelief. Was it possible?

"Anne Chambers? Please confirm for me that this is you."

Silence for a couple of seconds, then once again the box crackled to life. "…yes…"

Josh felt his heart leap back into his chest on its way to his throat. It was everything he'd ever hoped for, but he found himself a little confused as to what he should do next. He had so many questions, so many things he wanted to know, but common courtesy demanded that he at least get to know the spirit first before interrogating her.

"Hello, Anne. My name is…"

"…Josh…"

There could be no question now. How she knew his name, he didn't know, and frankly didn't care. The voice had spoken his name, and there was no way it was just coincidental. She had spoken his name intentionally, even cutting him off mid-sentence. There was no doubt in his mind that this was real, the real thing at last.

"Thank you for confirming your identity, Anne. I would like to have a chat with you if that's alright. We can talk about whatever you like."

"…yes…"

Josh's eyebrow cocked slightly. He was curious as to why Anne was seeming to answer in one-word sentences. "Why do you only say one word at a time, Anne?"

"…difficult…"

He nodded, though he wasn't sure if Anne could even see it. "I imagine it is. I'm sorry if I'm making things hard for you. Would it be easier if you just made this meter I'm holding flash? All you'd have to do is come near to it and it will detect you. Theoretically."

The lights on the EM meter began to blink, and Josh nodded once again. It was hard to contain his excitement, but for Anne's sake he just wanted to keep things casual, give her someone to talk with.

"Alright Anne, blink once for 'yes' and twice for 'no', alright?"

The meter blinked once. Josh smiled, hoping he was facing her. She might be a ghost, but she was still a human being to him. He wanted Anne to feel comfortable talking with him, trying not to obsess too much about her being dead and all.

"Anne, have you been here the whole time since you passed?"

One blink. Josh winced. It was difficult to imagine having to be stuck near one's own body after death, though he couldn't even begin to imagine why she would stay right here. Perhaps she simply had nowhere else to go, or perhaps she couldn't leave.

Perhaps she didn't want to go anywhere else.

"Do you not have anywhere else to go? Are you stuck here, unable to leave?"

Two blinks. Josh's eyebrow cocked again. She wasn't trapped in the cemetery, which wasn't necessarily a bad thing, but he still wondered why she would stay.

"Anne, I know it's difficult, but I need to ask you something that I really need you to tell me. Why would you stay here if you don't have to?"

Silence for a few seconds, but then the spirit box crackled back to life. "…sad…heartbroken…loss…"

"Someone hurt you?"

"…yes…"

"What happened?"

"…no…" The word sounded more emphatic somehow and was followed up by the spirit box flying two feet from its spot near the headstone. Josh found that his equipment was all losing power fast. The batteries were being drained. It seemed that he crossed a line that Anne didn't like, and Josh grimaced once again. He'd finally done it, finally opened a dialogue with the departed, and he pissed them off just like any other human being.

"I'm sorry, Anne. I didn't mean to pry into your personal business." Josh started to pick up his various bits of equipment, feeling extremely down on himself even in the face of his triumph. "I just…I dunno…I was excited that I finally was able to talk to someone. I've tried for a long time to speak with someone like you, and I go and do this. I am truly sorry. If you wish, I can come back another time, and we can talk about something else, if that's alright?"

Nothing for several seconds, but then, with the last of its power, the EM meter blinked once just before it shut off. Josh grinned slightly, though he still felt guilt over pushing too hard.

"Alright, Anne. I'll come back tomorrow night, and you can choose what we talk about, if that's okay."

"…yes…"

"Good night, Anne, and thank you."

There was nothing more, for the spirit box had run out of power too, but it was just as well. He'd managed to placate her for the moment, and got himself the first date he'd had in some time, though it was hardly a romantic one. It was amazing to know that he'd succeeded, but at the same time he knew that there was going to be a lot of hard work to come, if he was to track down Melissa. He did not want to use Anne to do it, but if it came down to it, he'd likely ask her if she was even aware of Melissa. He couldn't let anything get in the way of his ultimate goal.

Josh's day job was surprisingly mundane. He, like many people his age, stocked the shelves at a large grocery store. He enjoyed this work, primarily because he didn't really have to have much to do with the general public, except for the occasional question or a little help in tracking down a particular item. It wasn't that Josh wasn't friendly, or that he even minded dealing with people, but he preferred to keep his thoughts on what he truly considered to be his calling; working with the supernatural.

Also like many people his age, he had a

close-knit group of friends that thought his obsession with death and what might come after to be a touch unhealthy. His best friend was an excessively tall man who was named Albert, but preferred to go by "Al." Al was an intelligent young man who worked in an IT company. Al was a couple years older than Josh and had already graduated college, while Josh struggled to pass his classes.

Josh's group of friends also worried about his mental state. Another friend of his, a young lady named Heather, made no secret that she had designs on Josh, but she knew that Josh was in no way interested in any sort of romance. He just wasn't over Melissa and might never be. Still, where Josh went, Heather was generally there with him, being and doing everything that she could for him, desperately trying to help him hold his sanity together. Josh cared deeply for her, even if he didn't foresee romance. For the moment, Heather could accept that much.

The day after Josh's contact with Anne, he was back working and living the more mundane and banal parts of his life. As he was about to punch out for the day, he saw that Al and Heather had come by to collect him. He felt his heart leap just a little, at the thought of sharing the good news with his friends, but he wasn't sure if they'd even believe him. He intended to introduce them to Anne Chambers when the time was right, so that they could see that he wasn't insane. He wanted their faith in him, almost as much as he wanted to find his lost love. He needed them to believe him.

"Well, hello there," Heather said, smiling. "Long day?"

Josh grinned back, his eyes sparkling with happiness, something that neither of his close friends were used to seeing from him. "Nah. It was fine. I'm glad to see you two though."

Josh seemed in a good mood, which was evident to his friends. Though they worried, especially Al, that he was going down a dark path, one that was unravelling his sanity, he always seemed to hold it together. He had goals that he tried his best to hold on to, goals like graduating college, but after Melissa's death he seemed to lose all interest. It was good to see him lively and energetic again.

"You get laid or something, Josh?" Al asked, his rapier wit on point as always. "I can't think of any other explanation for this mood."

Josh laughed, another uncommon sight since Melissa's death. "No, it's just…nah, you wouldn't believe me if I told you."

"Try us," Heather said.

Josh shrugged and continued. "There's been a real breakthrough on my research. I did it! I managed to contact a real spirit!"

"Bullshit," Al chirped. "No such thing."

"I'm afraid you can't drag me down into your world of boring ass life, my friend. I know what I saw and what I heard."

Heather walked over to Josh and put her arm around him, her smile lighting up the immediate area. "I believe you, Josh."

"Thanks, H. It's real, and so is Anne."

"Anne?" Al skeptically asked. "Anne is…your

dead woman?"

"Well, she's not my woman. That would be weird. But yeah, she's the ghost I communicated with."

Heather's nose crinkled up. "How would that even work? A romance between a ghost and a living person?"

"Sounds like necrophilia to me," Al quipped. "Just another malfunction in your brain, pal."

Josh shook his head, though he still had a smile on his face. "Cast whatever aspersions you wish. I can *prove* this is real."

Josh received skeptical glares from his friends, but he quickly shrugged it off, causing them to relent. It was nearly impossible to change Josh's mind when he had it made up. No matter how his friends chided him, he held to what he knew was true, and there was no dissuading him.

Al slumped his shoulders and grinned. "Alright man. You show us that your ghost is real."

"Alright, naysayers, show up at the Irongate Cemetery tonight," Josh said, his smile radiant. "You'll see I'm right."

Heather put her arms around both Al and Josh, also smiling. "I'm hungry. Who's gonna buy me dinner?"

Josh laughed. "Guess I will."

"Alright then, lovebirds," Al chuckled. "You have fun. I'll be there tonight."

Josh blushed slightly at the comment. He'd never dated Heather, though he'd certainly thought about it more than once. The only reason he hadn't was simple; he'd met Melissa before anything could really blossom between him and Heather. Contrary to what he was sure that Al and Heather both thought, he knew full well that Heather was carrying a torch for him, but he was grateful that she was able to be his friend. She'd gotten him through the really hard times after Melissa's death, and he would always love her for that. He just had no room in his life for romance at that moment, even if it was ready-made and waiting for him.

Josh and Heather had a quick meal at their favorite local burger joint, a place called The Grease Pit. They discussed what was on their respective minds and had a good time, but something was definitely distracting Josh. All he could think about was returning to the cemetery and talking with Anne again. He didn't know why Anne took up so much of his attention; after all, this was only the beginning of their discourse. There was just something about the whole situation, the vindication he found in managing to contact the dead.

Night came, and Josh and Heather met up with Al at the gate to Irongate Cemetery. Josh was more excited about this night than anything in recent memory. He knew, beyond any question, that he was going to change his friends' lives. He was going to prove that life existed beyond death, the ultimate answer to the ultimate philosophical question.

Josh took point, leading the others to the gravesite. Anne's headstone was the same as it had been; surrounded by weeds and worn over the decades. No one had been there to care for her grave besides the cemetery groundskeepers. Josh couldn't help but think that would be the loneliest existence imaginable, to linger forever, always alone, never finding companionship again. Josh couldn't imagine his life without his friends, but Anne had no friends, or family, or anyone at all.

Heather was constantly looking over her shoulder. "Guys…I don't think we should be here," she said, her voice trembling.

Al snickered. "Surely you don't believe that there's something out to get you, do you?"

"Not everyone is as much of an atheist as you, Al," Heather snapped back. "Some people believe that there's something more after death, even if we don't know what it is."

"Superstitionist nonsense," Al commented.

"Y'all shut up," Josh interjected. "We're there."

The three young people made a loose semicircle around the front of the grave. Josh laid out the various devices that he'd used before, carefully setting them in front of the headstone. The EM meter immediately began to blink weakly, and the smile on Josh's face widened. Even if the others were skeptical, he knew… Anne was there.

"Hello, Anne," Josh said, in a hushed, almost reverent tone.

Nothing happened besides a mild flicker on the EM meter. Al's eyebrow raised in impatience, wondering just when Josh's so-called "evidence" was going to reveal itself. Heather began to violently shiver, as if the temperature had just dropped thirty degrees.

"Guys…I really don't think we should be here," Heather said, her voice trembling.

"No, it's okay," Josh emphatically spoke. "She's uncertain about your intentions. She wasn't expecting anyone but me."

"Uncertain?" Al asked, his voice dripping with smarm. "What are we going to do, kill her?"

"…no…" A single word, clear as a bell, came out of the spirit box. Everyone immediately fell silent, certainly not expecting any kind of response.

"Anne?" Josh called out. "I'm sorry if you weren't prepared to have other guests. These are my friends, Al, and Heather. They'd like to meet you, just like I did."

The crackle of static seemed to physically fill the air around them, almost as if a current were running through the very air itself, electrifying anything it touched. Everyone stared at the little device, afraid to speak, afraid to do anything but blink.

"…no…"

Heather turned the palest shade of white. "You guys…that thing spoke."

"Should we leave, Anne?" Josh asked.

Heather nodded wholeheartedly, and Al just stood there, silent. A moment passed, then a full minute. There was nothing but static.

"Okay," Al said, nearly in a whisper. "This is fucked up. Josh, please tell me that you're fucking with us."

"No," said Josh. "I'm not."

"…no…"

Everyone sighed with relief. The last thing that anyone needed to deal with was an angry ghost with a vendetta for no reason beyond their presence.

"…you…"

Josh stepped forward a half-step. "Me? What about me? Do you want only me to stay?"

"…yes…"

"No problem," Al said, his voice beginning to tremble. "We're out of here."

"…Josh…"

"No," Heather began to mutter. "No, no, no, no, *no*! This is messed-up, it's wrong! This is a sick joke, Josh."

"…Josh…not…joking…"

Everyone's attention was fully on the box. Josh was nervous but elated; Anne had been able to say more than one word at a time. Al began to take on a similar complexion to Heather's deathly pale, as he felt the very blood drain away from his face. It flew in the face of everything sensible, but everyone knew that Josh was not the kind for vicious pranks. He certainly would not try to frighten them like this.

But the alternative possibility was far, far worse.

"I'm sorry," Heather said, her voice quaking with dread. "I can't do this anymore, Josh, I'm sorry. I'm leaving."

Josh saw out of the corner of his eye that Heather was fixated on the equipment sitting in front of her. Josh remained fixated as well; he found himself desperately wanting Anne to say more, to tell him what he truly wanted to know. The answer was right there, right in front of him, dangling tantalizingly from a stick held by God-only-knows-what. But even then, it was still *just* out of reach.

"…please…Josh…"

Josh started to share his comrades' dread as Anne's phantasmal vocabulary grew before his eyes. He knew that the voice over the spirit box was more of a synthetic product than would have been her actual voice, and yet he could almost hear a desperation in her voice, a fear of her own. Everything he knew, that he truly felt that he knew, told him that she wasn't crying out to him, and that her malaise could not actually be transmissible.

What he saw, though, and what he *felt*, told him Anne needed him there.

Al and Heather both backed away, and when they'd reached a suitable distance, they turned and fled as fast as they could. Josh remained there, his attention fully on Anne.

"I'm sorry," Josh whispered. "I should have checked with you first before bringing my friends."

"It is…alright…Josh…"

Slowly sitting upon the ground before the headstone, Josh folded his legs underneath himself, trying to get comfortable on the hard ground. It had been several decades since Anne had been buried, and the earth around her in time became compacted. Only the few weeds and grasses around her grave could grow there now. A single tear welled up in Josh's eye as he thought about the existential loneliness at Anne had endured for nearly a century.

"Can you…manifest yourself? Appear to me? Sit and talk with me for a while?"

"…difficult…"

"If you need some kind of energy to do it, then take what you need from me," Josh said. "Whatever you need."

The air temperature dropped sharply. Josh's breath became visible. He felt something vital siphoning from him, but he did not resist. He needed to see, to know. If Anne was capable of appearing to him, then he could know for certain that this was all real, and that there was a very real chance that Melissa was still around, in some fashion.

A strange mist began to swirl around the grave, appearing from nothing. The mist formed itself into a roughly humanoid shape, though tendrils still swirled around the grave, even touching Josh. The mist felt like the very cold of death itself and he knew real fear. He didn't want to fear her, but a primal terror took him, as he tried to back away from the rapidly coalescing mist figure.

And then, as quickly as it had begun, the mist was completely consumed by a female figure. She was striking, in a long, blue dress that was cinched in the middle by a wide belt. Her dark brown hair was cut just above her chin and curled slightly towards the front. She was also surprisingly young, even though Josh knew she was only twenty when she died. She was not at all what he expected, and there was something else that troubled him.

He could feel more tears fall down his face. He was feeling something he hadn't felt in so long, since the loss of Melissa. His jaw went slack as he took in the totality of her manifestation. The woman from another time smiled a smile so genuine and honest it hit Josh like a physical force.

"Hello, Josh," she said, not through any electronic device, but with her own voice.

"Hey, Anne," he replied, trying to maintain his cool even though the opposing forces of care and terror waged war within his mind. "I…didn't know that you were so…"

"Human?" she asked, her smile raising slightly in one corner of her mouth. "I suppose that's true. What made me who I was is still here, somehow, and has been since my death."

"Beautiful…" Josh finished.

Anne continued to smile, but she turned slightly away. "You're just saying that."

"I…I'm sorry, I just…" Josh struggled to speak, but no words would come.

"I have been so lonely, Josh, for so long. Then along comes someone who wants to speak with me, someone who thinks I'm beautiful…"

"I mean, yeah…I'm sure you were very lonely. But that's over with. I'm here now, and I will come back as often as you want. I want to get to know you, Anne."

"Dear Joshua…be careful what you wish for."

Anne, seeming to almost glide over to Josh, ran the back of her hand down Josh's cheek. To his surprise, it felt quite solid, and nowhere as cold as he'd thought it would be. She smiled radiantly as she peered into his eyes. Her deep pools of blue seemed to pull Josh in. He was entranced, completely under her bewitchment. She placed a gentle kiss on his forehead, and then rose once more.

"Go home, Josh," she said. "I am becoming quite tired."

"I'll be back tomorrow night."

"Don't worry about that. We will see each other again soon."

The mist unzipped from the figure as she became hazy, translucent, and it swirled around her as she vanished before his eyes. Josh's heart pounded with excitement and fear. What had she done to him? Was it possible? Could someone be attracted to a dead woman like that? Was it just the excitement of the moment that had become a facsimile of attraction? He did not know, and he found thinking about it chilled his soul. He silently gathered his equipment and left the graveyard, excited but confused.

Josh lay in his bed that night, looking up at the ceiling. He became angrier with himself with every passing moment. How could he have forgotten Melissa so quickly? Yes, while it was true that Melissa was dead, so was Anne! What he was feeling, he hadn't felt about Melissa since coming to terms with her absence, even though he tried so hard to find her, reach her. But he hadn't felt such raging passion for Melissa since about six months after her death, and he felt it now.

Was it really wrong? Maybe, but he felt it, nonetheless.

Even at work the next day, this quandary perplexed and enraged him. He was distracted, irritable, sluggish, and everyone around him could see it. Some worried that it was a relapse of the severe depression he'd felt at the time of Melissa's death, but this time it was far worse than that. It was rage at himself for forgetting such a wonderful woman so quickly. He had mourned, and in many ways still did mourn, but it didn't feel like enough to him. After all, it was because of his overpowering desire to find Melissa that he'd gotten into ghost hunting, though there was always a part of him, one of the last shreds of logic left in a mind powered by desperation and obsession, that hadn't really expected to find anything.

He had found something, however, and found himself intensely attracted to her.

His mind occupied while climbing a ladder, Josh fell. Panic filled him, but shortly before he hit the ground, something slowed his fall. Amazed he wasn't injured, he picked himself up off of the ground and looked around. There was no one there, but he knew he had felt someone's hands catch him.

What in the Hell is going on? If there was no one there to catch him, then clearly it was something unseen, and there was only one candidate that qualified. A chill ran down his spine as he realized that somehow, Anne had left the graveyard and had followed him to work. A surge of fear and revulsion ripped through his stomach as he processed the thought. Was Anne following him, or was it all just coincidence? Had he just fallen and landed softly enough to not harm himself? Questions flooded his mind, all swirling about in a whorl of terror.

"Anne?" he whispered, not expecting a response.

A can of soup that he had knocked off of the shelf when he fell slowly rolled towards him. He knelt down to pick it up, the spirit's presence all but confirmed. Her being there caused even more questions to enter his mind, not the least of which was wondering why she had followed him. Perhaps it was only because she was lonely and wanted instead to spend her time with him. It also could mean that she entertained an affection, or possibly even an attraction, for him. She was a person, after all. Could a ghost feel attraction like a living person did?

He shook his head, trying to rid himself of the thoughts he was having that were borderline blasphemy. It was insane to even entertain such thoughts, or so he kept trying to tell himself, but he could almost *feel* her there, and it was comforting in a way that didn't quite sit well with him. *No*, he thought, *I have to get this whole crazy idea out of my mind.* Everything logical within him told him that there was no way that it could work, and instead end up disastrous for both of them, and in his view, Anne had definitely already been through enough for two.

The end of the day inevitably came, and Josh punched out and prepared to head home, but he couldn't get Anne out of his mind. She had appeared so beautifully to him, like some kind of goddess from another era, and he could not prevent himself from thinking about her. Every time his mind went idle, the image of her perfect face filled his every conscious thought, and it was becoming more than just a nuisance. He was even considering discussing the idea of a living/dead couple with Anne, and such a thing…well, it defied common sense and morality. It was possibly even illegal, even if he was never actually touching the corpse, which would remain safely interred in its grave in perpetuity.

"Hey," a voice ripped through the reverie.

Outside the employee door, Heather stood waiting for him. He looked at her and smiled, for it was good to have a person to think about that wasn't going to drive him over the edge. She was dressed well, better than her usual t-shirt and jeans combo, and she had put on makeup. She tended towards the more gothic style when she chose to, and it looked good on her. Josh found himself wondering what would happen if he were to give a relationship with Heather a try. Certainly, it made more sense than dating a woman who'd been dead for a century.

"Something on your mind, Josh?" asked Heather. Her smile belied a concern that was clear in her eyes.

"I just…I guess I wasn't expecting to see you so soon, after the scare last night," said Josh. "I thought you'd be too spooked to want to hang out."

Heather giggled, in the cute way she always did. "No, not really. I mean, sure, it was scary, but it's not like the ghost is following you or anything, right?"

Josh blinked. "Uh…no. She's probably still in the cemetery." He hoped he didn't sound too much like the inexperienced liar that he was.

"I don't know, maybe it would be cool to have a ghost friend, right? Someone who could always have your back and no one would ever know it."

"I…I don't know about that," Josh managed to stammer out. "Hey, Heather, wait a second. I want to ask you something."

Heather stopped in her tracks, turned to him, and cocked her head slightly. "Sure. What's up?"

Josh closed his eyes, and inhaled deeply,

gathering the courage to continue. "Do you wanna go out sometime?"

Heather's eyes narrowed, even though her smile was unchanged. "You mean like on a date?"

"Yeah," Josh replied. "Exactly like that."

Heather moved closer to him, wrapping her arms around his waist, and kissing him softly on the cheek. "I thought you'd never ask. When?"

"Tomorrow night too soon?"

"I'll be ready and waiting at seven," Heather chirped, clearly elated.

A loud sound suddenly broke out from behind them, like something hitting a metal sign. Both of them turned sharply to see where the noise had come from, seeing nothing behind them but a stop sign that seemed to be swaying as if it had been hit. Heather's eyes widened, but there seemed to be no fear behind them, whereas Josh seemed truly startled. His eyes darted around, looking for some other sign of the presence he'd forgotten about in the moment, but he saw nothing. If Anne was there, she hadn't chosen to manifest herself. Heather knelt down and saw what appeared to be a small bird that had accidentally flown into the sign.

"Oh, the poor thing," she said. "I hope it's going to be okay."

Josh sighed with relief, but the situation warranted him being a little more cautious about what he said and did when there could be an invisible presence watching his every move. He did care about Heather and did want to explore the possibilities of a relationship with her, but he had to think about Anne's feelings as well. It was something that he would need to discuss with the ghost; he needed to know exactly where she stood with him.

Heather walked with Josh all the way to his home, and they enjoyed a hug before saying their goodbyes. He went inside, and, seeing that there was no one home, took a deep breath, trying to figure out how best to approach the situation.

"Hello, Josh," Anne's voice spoke from behind him, making him jump from fright.

"Jesus, Anne, don't do that!" he snapped, mostly from embarrassment.

"I'm sorry," she said. "I just wanted to welcome you home."

"How are you even here? I thought you were stuck at the cemetery." He turned to face the place the voice was coming from, and there, fully manifest, stood Anne, a broad smile on her face.

"No, silly, I can go wherever I want," she replied. "I just stayed there because I had nowhere else to go, and there are others there as lonely as I was."

"Was?"

Anne drew closer and placed her arms around his neck, pulling him in close to her. "Then you came along."

Josh pulled away from her embrace, trying to sort through his own emotions, never mind comprehending hers. "This…this is something we need to talk about."

"I agree," Anne replied. "It's past time we discussed our feelings for each other."

Josh sat down on a chair in the living room and gestured for Anne to take a seat on the sofa, out of the range for physical contact. She did so, though a look of confusion seemed to cross her delicate features. Josh couldn't help but stare. Anne was one of the most beautiful women he'd ever seen, without question, but he had no idea how a relationship with her could work. Besides, he worried that whatever business kept her in this world, at least according to common lore, would be interfered with by his getting together with her.

"I…I am definitely attracted to you," Josh said.

"As I am to you, dearest," Anne spoke, her voice becoming oddly quiet. "You are in every way a better man than my husband was."

"Your husband?"

Anne nodded, a sad look in her eyes. "He was an awful man, but he was the one my parents believed was the right choice for me. They could not have been more wrong, Josh. It was that awful man that…"

Her words trailed off, but Josh knew exactly what she was telling him; her husband, whoever this Mr. Chambers may have been, killed her. A surge of sorrow, a palpable, physical force, washed over him as realization had set in. Anne had been murdered at such a young age that she'd missed out on a lot of life. It was a terrible feeling, but it only seemed to strengthen the emotions that he felt for her.

Anne collected herself and continued. "Regardless, you are a hundred times the man he ever was. Since you came into my l…well, you know… things have been so very different. You've given me a reason to exist, something worth the passion of my heart, and I feel…well, I feel that I love you."

It was as if those words slapped Josh across his dumbfounded face. He had no idea how to respond to such a declaration, nor did he know how best to proceed from there. It was of no consequence, however, because after a couple of seconds of silence, Anne rose from her seat and approached him. She climbed into his lap, straddling him, and kissed him passionately. It was the most intense feeling that Josh had ever experienced, and deep down, within his most primal self, he wanted more. He didn't care that she was dead, and he wasn't, nor did he even think about what this could mean with Heather. He gave himself fully to the goddess on him in that moment, and there was nothing else but Josh and Anne. There was no death, there was no anything but the two of them.

"Anne…" Josh whispered as the kiss ended.

"You don't need to speak, my love," Anne whispered back to him. "Just be here with me right now."

He didn't speak. He couldn't, and he didn't want to. He just wanted more. He kissed her with equal passion, abandoning all thought except for thoughts of her. Nothing else mattered to him.

Josh lay in bed that night, looking up at the ceiling as usual. The only difference this time was that he was actually happy for the first time in a long time. Though he'd only known Anne a short while, he felt as if they'd known each other for years. It no longer bothered him that she didn't breathe, or that he could never hear her heartbeat, because after their intimate moment, he knew beyond any doubt that Anne was the woman for him. In truth, she was the best possible choice for him. She would never grow old, and she would never die, if only because she was already dead. Though he still thought about Melissa, he just came to the assumption that not all dead people knew every other dead person; there were so many that had died over the millennia that such a notion was impossible. Melissa had gone on to whatever her fate was, and he could find peace with that.

What of Heather, though? They were supposed to have a date together the next night, and he fully intended to go through with it, but how could he ever explain that he was in a committed relationship with the dead woman who had terrified her so? In addition to that, how was Anne supposed to feel about it? Surely she would not be fine with him dating another woman.

It was truly the logistics of the situation that made dating a dead woman so inconvenient.

"What is on your mind, my love?" Anne whispered from next to him. He didn't jump, but he was somewhat startled by the sudden words. When he turned to see where the words had come from, he found Anne in bed next to him, slowly snaking her arms around him and snuggling in close.

"I…made a promise to someone, that we would go out and have a fun evening," he said, omitting anything about any blossoming romance between himself and Heather. "I'm concerned about it because, well, I worry about what you would think."

"That Heather girl?"

"Yeah," Josh continued. "We made plans for tomorrow night, but I don't want you thinking that there's anything to worry about."

"I'm not worried," she said, laying her head upon his chest. "I know you won't be like that bastard husband of mine. You won't betray me, will you, Josh?"

"No, never! It's just…I don't want you having to see me out with another woman."

Anne giggled, clearly amused. "Darling, contrary to what you believe, I do not follow you everywhere. I won't follow you and Heather, either. You deserve your privacy, and I trust you. Shouldn't I?"

"You should, but I didn't want to keep this from you."

Anne raised herself on her arms, looking straight into his eyes. "It's appreciated." She kissed him gently, and then dissipated into the mist once again.

Josh tucked his hands under his head, a big, dumb grin on his face. It was all so simple; he would just draw the line at anything romantic and/or sexual. He wouldn't have to cheat on Anne, and he wouldn't have to feel like he was leading Heather on. It was all going to work out just fine. He drifted off to sleep, his dreams only of his beloved.

Josh found the next day at work went by like lightning, and before he knew it, it was five o'clock and time to clock out. His smile hadn't faded throughout the day, even though he knew that his date with Heather was rapidly approaching. He found himself wishing that he hadn't actually made the date, if only so that he could have more time with Anne. He got home and hopped in the shower quickly, trying get himself presentable. Even if he wasn't wholeheartedly invested in the date, there was no reason for Heather to know that, or at least so he rationalized. He felt unseen eyes on him from just the other side of the shower curtain, and he smiled.

"Is that you, Anne?" he asked, hoping that it

was.

A pale hand reached inside the shower and grabbed his hand. This only accentuated Josh's smile.

"Why don't you join me?" Josh asked.

"You know full well where that will lead, darling," Anne's voice whispered from right behind him.

Josh's grin became slightly wry as the tingle from Anne's whisper propagated throughout his body. Her very presence was getting him hard, and he desperately wanted to take her right there, in the shower. "And if that's my plan all along?"

An invisible force turned him around 180 degrees, and his eyes met Anne's. The deep blue of her eyes seemed to pull him in, but he was acutely aware that she was as naked as he was. Her body was shapely in every way that he liked, and it only made his erection swell. She was so perfect, so wondrous…he submitted completely to her will. She wrapped her arms around him, pulling him closer, and began to kiss him with great fervor. Josh found himself wanting desperately to get out of his date with Heather, and instead spend the whole time in the shower, making love with Anne.

In the town library, Al was busy searching for something. He'd gotten a bad feeling from the beginning about this phantasmal love interest of Josh's, so he ran through dozens of microfilms of old newspapers, looking for something, anything that would give him some clue as to who Anne Chambers actually was. After about an hour of searching, he found exactly what he was looking for, even if it was nowhere close to what he expected.

The headline for December Thirty-first, 1923, in bold print, read "Local Woman Dies in Asylum". As Al read through the article, he became more and more horrified as to what he saw. It said that a woman named Anne Chambers, whose date of death matched the headstone where everything had happened, had attempted to kill her husband, failed, and was arrested. At her trial, she had been found criminally insane and was committed to Ravenvale Asylum, where she eventually hanged herself.

"Jesus," Al muttered quietly. "I have got to tell Josh about this."

He made a quick printout of the newspaper page, and dashed out of the library, hoping beyond hope that he wasn't too late.

At seven o'clock, almost on the dot, a knock came at Heather's door, which she answered almost immediately, as she was waiting near the door for Josh to show up. She was glad that he was actually going through with it, as she wasn't sure that she could forgive him if he flaked out on her. She opened the door to see Josh, all cleaned up and dressed nicely, and a wide smile on his face.

"Ready?" he asked.

"Yeah, let's go!" she exclaimed, her exuberance taking control.

Josh grinned as Heather clambered into the passenger's seat of Josh's rusty old Escort, and they headed off. He drove her to the north side of town, where all the good stores and restaurants were, and pulled into the parking lot at Giovanni's, the premier Italian place in town. This caused Heather to smile as broadly as Josh because Giovanni's wasn't cheap. Surely this was an indication that he was genuinely interested.

They were seated fairly quickly and handed menus. The waitress was an exceptionally polite young woman that had a smile much like the one that Josh, and Heather had. They placed their orders, and the waitress disappeared into the back of the house.

"So…here we are!" Heather said, pleased.

"Yes," Josh said. "We are here." He chuckled at that, trying to stay as friendly as possible.

"What changed your mind, Josh?" she asked.

"I don't know. I guess all this stuff with ghosts and whatnot just sort of…let me know that somehow, it's okay to let go of Melissa. And, if I can be really honest, I've always had something of a thing for you, even if we didn't really have our chance until now. I don't know, really. I *do* know that it's the right time."

"Shit, you mean it's *about* time," Heather quipped. "I've been waiting for you to get your head back on straight for years." She giggled, not trying to be mean-spirited.

"Okay, that's fair," he replied. "There wasn't anything about you I didn't like, it's just…I don't know…grief is complicated."

"I'll give you that."

"So…what do you want to do on our date?" Josh asked.

"I say…let's take in a movie and after that…" she said, leaning closer. "Rage fucking for hours. I have a lot of pent-up frustration that I need to get out."

"Whoa, whoa, slow it down, girl," Josh said.

"Don't you think that's moving a little fast?"

"No, not really."

"I like the movie idea. As for the rest, let's just…see what the night brings."

Heather grinned wryly at Josh, though her eyes betrayed a lust that she was determined to satisfy. She raised her water glass towards him. "To what the night brings."

Al knocked furiously on Josh's door, but there was no answer. "Josh, dude, I need to talk to you. It's about your ghost…she's not exactly as advertised, you get me?"

The door opened, albeit slowly, and Al walked in to the apartment. There was clearly no one there, but there was a humidity to the place that suggested Josh had showered recently. He'd just missed him, and that was a bad thing. Al looked around one final time, but saw no sign that Josh was still there, and so turned back to the door.

"Can I help you?" Seemingly from out of nowhere, a woman stood in front of the door, dressed only in one of Josh's t-shirts. She looked angry, as if she'd been interrupted by him.

"Yeah…" he said, startled by the sudden appearance of the woman. "I'm looking for Josh."

"He's not here."

"Yeah, no shit," Al replied. "Where's he at?"

"I don't see how that's any of your business. If you want, I can pass him a message when he comes home.”

Suddenly, Al's mind came to a horrifying revelation, one that chilled him to his very soul. “You…you're not Anne, are you?”

The corner of her mouth turned upwards in a wicked grin. “And if I am?”

“How is this even possible? You're…”

“Dead?” the woman spat. “You silly mortals. You have no idea what's there beyond the passage of death, and yet you search so fervently for the answers that you can never truly find.”

“Okay, settle down, Anne,” Al said, warily raising his hands in front of him. “I did no such thing.”

“But you did, at my grave, with Josh and Heather. It was so rude of you to run away from me. A woman might think that you had a problem with them.”

“Yeah, I do. I know how you died, and where.”

Anne cocked her head to the side, her expression becoming more curious than angry. “Do you now?”

“Yeah, and I'm gonna make sure he knows *everything*.”

Anne laughed, a cold, predatory laugh, and then waved her hand towards Al. With a horrific crunch, his neck twisted nearly completely away from his torso, and he slumped to the ground, as dead as she was.

“No, you're not.”

She quickly discorporated into mist and vanished out the open door.

“So…I've been thinking,” Heather said. “Why don't we just sorta…skip the movie and just head back to your place. We can…play.”

“Oh no, we…umm…can't go to my place,” Josh blurted out in desperation. “I have…company.”

“Do you? I didn't know about that.”

“I don't tell you *everything* that goes on in my life, you know.”

“Josh, are you trying to avoid being alone with me?”

Josh turned nearly as pale as his ghostly mistress. “What…what do you mean?”

Heather narrowed her eyes at him, frustration beginning to boil up once again. “You are not the sort to turn down easy, commitment-less sex. At least you've never done it before, but now you're making shit up to not be alone with me. I guess my question is why?”

“I…I…I just don't want to fuck this one up, Heather,” Josh managed to stutter out. “Most women I date, I don't have the history with them that I do with you. Does that make any sense? I'm not trying to use you for sex, so if that means we hold off for a bit just to make sure this is going to work, then I'm cool with it.”

“Joshua…” Heather said, taking his hand and stroking it gently. “I think I'm understanding you, but I'm ready when you are. I think it's sweet that you're thinking about me, but you don't have to worry. Let's just play it by ear in that case.”

"Thank you," Josh said, smiling once again. "This, you and me, means something, and I don't want to ruin that."

The waitress reappeared with their food, and they ate quietly, their glances doing the talking. They finished equally quickly and departed after Josh paid the bill. They drove back to Heather's apartment, a few miles from Josh's place, and settled in to get comfortable. Josh sat down on the love seat, in front of the television, and relaxed until Heather sat down beside him. They'd sat together on this love seat several times in the past, but never had there been such an internal struggle on Josh's part before. On one hand, he had someone he dearly loved, that being Anne, but there was also Heather, who clearly loved him, and wasn't asking for any sort of commitment. He was confused, and that wasn't a good thing.

Heather placed her hand on his thigh, the wicked smile reappearing on her face. Josh felt a surge of panic run up his spine, but at the same time enjoyed it. Heather knew all his weaknesses and secrets, and she would be exploiting them all. He knew he was asking for trouble if he came to Heather's place, but he couldn't…

Heather leaned in close and kissed him, only once, gently. A second passed as Josh's mind was overridden, but they embraced tightly and kissed each other with zeal.

Suddenly, without any warning, Heather began to scream in terror and pain, recoiling away from him hard. Tears flowed profusely down her cheeks as she writhed in agony due to some unseen assailant. Blood began to seep through the cloth of her black top, and she fell to the floor, clutching her abdomen.

"Heather?" Josh impotently shouted in shock.

"What's wrong?"

Heather slowly pulled up the bottom of the black top she was wearing, and there, in horrible scratch marks that looked like the work of some vicious animal, was spelled out the word "WHORE". Josh's eyes opened wide at the sight, and within seconds he knew who was responsible for the terrible attack on Heather. He scooped Heather up, intending to carry her out of the apartment and to a hospital, but was met with an invisible wall of force that slammed into him and knocked them both to the floor.

Josh tried to pick himself up off of the floor, but was once again hit with an invisible attack, one that set his head spinning and made his field of vision grow dim for a moment. He slumped down onto the floor, and everything went black.

"Wake up, darling." A wicked voice cut through the silent void. "Open your eyes."

Josh did as he was told, though there was extreme pain in his head as he struggled to open what felt like horribly swollen eyelids. Everywhere Josh could see there was blood, splattered all over the room and dripping from a table in front of him. He had never seen so much blood at one time, and he gulped in horror when he realized from where the blood had come.

On the table in front of him, tied down by the hands and feet, was what remained of Heather, almost completely eviscerated, and her vital organs splayed around, some on the floor and some still hanging from the horrific wound by a strand of viscera. He tried to scream, but he was gagged, and no sound came out. A terrible laugh rang out, one that sounded truly unholy and echoed off of the walls. It was only then that Josh realized that they were in almost total darkness, the only light coming from candles around the room. There seemed to be no one else in the room.

"Hello? Anne?" Josh cried out, terrified beyond words.

"I am here, my love."

"Why? Why have you done this?" he asked, desperation growing in his voice.

"Do you not know? She wants to take you away from me, and I can't allow that. I can't let you be like my husband. He was a terrible, terrible man." The voice of Anne, disembodied, seemed to come from everywhere around him, making him feel confined, trapped. "You're not a bad man, are you Josh? No…no, it was that Jezebel that did it, that lured you in. And she has paid for it, my love, I promise you."

A straight razor seemed to lift into the air and float over to Josh's neck. It stopped just above Josh's carotid artery and hovered there.

"No, she can't take you away now," the voice continued. "Just like your friend Al can't stop us from being together."

"You…killed Al? Why?" Josh pled.

"He was a liar!" Something in the distance seemed to smash against some hard surface, shattering loudly. Josh jumped at the sound, terrified for his life. "They're all liars! They don't understand you like I do, Josh! They just want to take you away from me, but that's okay."

Mist swirled around him, slowly coalescing into the familiar figure of Anne. She held the razor delicately in her right hand, and she had a terrible smile on her face, one akin to that of a crocodile. She leaned in close, so close she was almost pressed up against him, and ran the razor down the length of his face. He struggled to get free, but he knew that it would not avail him of anything.

In a hushed whisper, Anne spoke. "I will make sure we are always together, darling."

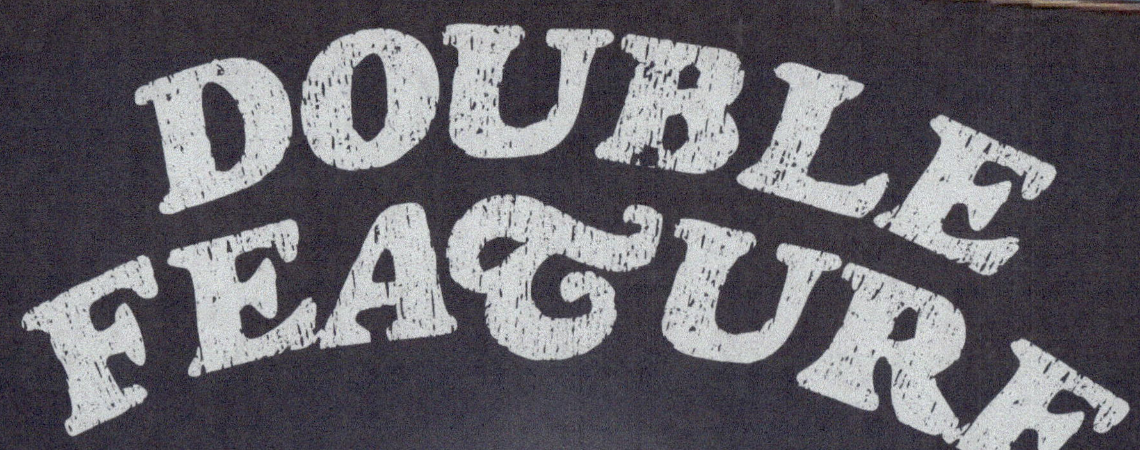
DOUBLE FEATURE
YEAR TWO PREVIEW

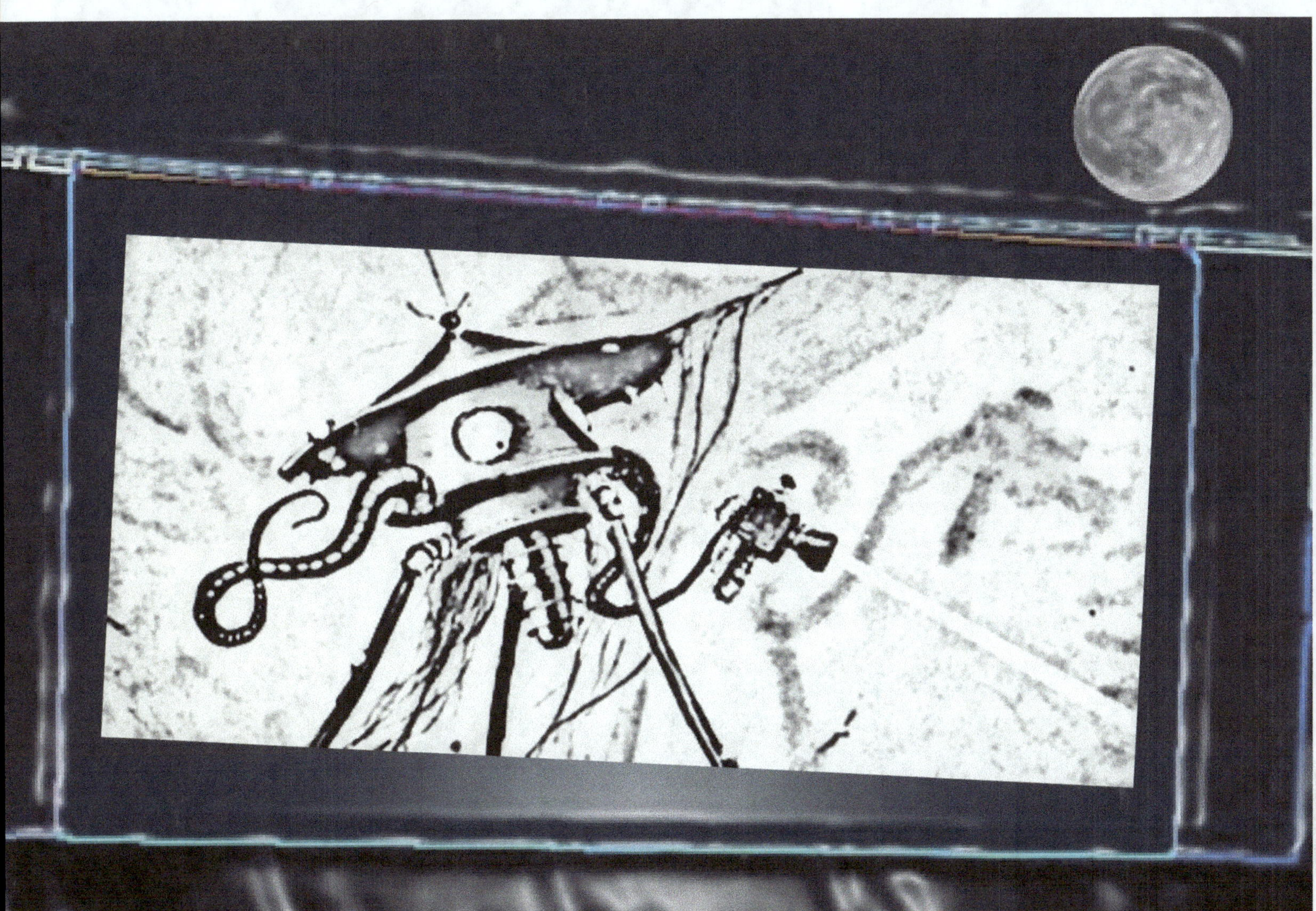

Double Feature #5: 50's SCI-FI w/ John A. McColley

Double Feature #6:
Wilderness Terror
w/ DS Vernon

Double Feature ANNUAL #2: HOME with HAMMER

SHIFT CHANGE

John A. McColley

"You say this is fully organic? No pesticides, no toxic fertilizers leaching into the soil?" Simon asked the server, looking over the plate of vegetables dressed in brown sauce over quinoa. The server nodded. "It's absolutely delicious."

"I'll be sure to pass your compliments along."

"I'd like to do so myself, if that's all right. I'm a bit of a foodie, and would love to pick his brain regarding the menu for an upcoming dinner party."

"I'm afraid the chef is quite busy tonight, as every night." The server waved a hand at the rest of the dining room. The tables were packed, conversation and wine flowing freely. Still, Simon wanted to quiz the creator of such a meal about their process, both for preparing and obtaining such produce. Nothing in the shops compared.

Paying for his meal, he went into the bathroom and waited for shift change, or close up, or whatever they called it here. As the sounds of dining and cooking dropped off, he began picking his feet up in the stall whenever the door opened. Eventually, he heard muffled yelling back and forth between the front room and kitchen. Cecil's was closing. Self conscious, the threat of being caught producing butterflies in his stomach, Simon crept to the bathroom door, listening intently. Metal rang lightly on metal as someone gathered mixing bowls, cookware, and utensils for washing.

Simon slowly pushed the door open, peering out. He saw no one, but the sounds of cleaning up in the kitchen persisted. He slipped into the hall and up to the swinging kitchen doors. Taking a deep breath, he steeled himself for the meeting. Would the man have him arrested? He would have to be convincing to argue against that. Would it be worth even that to meet *the Cecil?* Absolutely.

Finally, he pushed the door open and stepped through in case anyone was still at the front of the house and saw him down the short hallway. "Cecil, I presume. I know you're busy, but I wanted to congratulate you on…" His voice stuck in his throat as the white-clothed figure turned and he saw the others' face… and neck… and hands…

"You presume much, young one," the other's voice creaked.

"What happened to-"

"Are you here to talk about food, or my disfigurement?" Cecil asked, looking back to his work, scraping the fry surface, directing unidentifiable crisped bits and scorched grease to a rectangular hole.

"I'm sorry, Chef. Perhaps I should go."

"It's too late for that now," Cecil said.

"Pardon?" Simon asked, the hair on the back of his neck raising.

"You've already been traumatized by my appearance. You'll never eat at those tables out there again."

"I wouldn't say-" Simon began to object, but he knew it was true. Seeing the splotchy lumps, some bloodless, white, others deep red, almost like ripe fruit, drove the idea of ever eating again from Simon's mind.

"Come, I was about to make myself some dinner. Let us chat." Simon *had* gone through all this trouble to meet the chef, and his food *was* amazing…

"Shu-" he croaked, his throat suddenly dry. He swallowed hard. "Sure, Chef, that sounds great."

Cecil lit a burner on the gas stove top just over from the fry top and pulled down a cast iron skillet. Simon watched from the far side of a twenty foot long island running down the middle of the space as Chef scooped a ball of lard from a canister on the counter beside the stove and let it sizzle in the pan while he rocked it, causing the ball to roll all around the heated surface. Soon, the smell of hot grease took on sharp spicy notes.

"Rosemary, thyme, mint, and marjoram," Cecil said, though Simon hadn't seen the chef add the herbs. "Let's see, you had the…" Chef sniffed, "Vegetable quinoa medley. Are you a vegetarian, ehh…?"

"Simon. Not always, but I wanted something lighter. My lunch turned out to be heavier than I had expected. Who knew I had to plan the day's meals around my reservation at Cecil's?"

"Ah, planning, yes, especially meals, is very important. Perhaps you are… not ready?"

"I am, Chef, please, teach me everything!" Simon said, hands splayed on the island, voice rising.

"Mmm…" Cecil sounded uncertain. "You are not Jewish, or Muslim? You can eat pork?"

"No, I'm not- I mean, I love pork, and bacon-" Cecil snorted at this.

"Everyone's so obsessed with bacon these days. It's a real pain in the ass, you know? There are other parts of a pig. Juicy, succulent parts."

"Of course, Chef," Simon acknowledged. Who knew the man would be so opinionated about meats? But then, it did make sense. A chef of Cecil's caliber had to have discerning tastes, strong attractions to certain foods, and likely aversions to others.

While these thoughts occupied his mind, Simon missed Cecil retrieving the meat and setting it in the pan. The sizzle rose dramatically.

"I find the juxtaposition of beef notes and pork gives the meat a special flavor. Much like the onions and apples I've sliced into the lard." Onions? Simon could smell them, but didn't recall Cecil retrieving them or cutting them, or any apples. "Plate?" Cecil

asked, turning and looking meaningfully down at the island. Simon looked down and saw the side of the long counter had doors. Within, he found stacks of dinner plates, cream colored, shallow, uniform. He pulled one from the nearest stack and lay it on the steel surface close to the chef.

Rather than turning with the skillet and moving the pork onto the plate where it lay, Cecil took the plate and worked, actions blocked out by the lumpy wall of white his jacket represented. When he turned back around, there lay four perfectly cooked medallions with the lightest sear distributed across most of the visible sides in an arc along the right side of the plate, drizzled with the jus and seeming to cup the browned apples and onions. As Chef pushed the plate across the counter, Simon noted a glint of gold amid the protrusions that had once been fingers. Cecil had been married. Simon began to wonder what had happened to leave the man like this when the scent of the food invaded his mind, focusing him elsewhere.

"It smells amazing. It *looks* amazing!" Simon enthused, his mouth watering despite having just eaten. Cecil held out a fork.

"Have at it." Simon took the fork, cutting the first medallion with the side of the tines with almost no effort. When he brought it to his mouth, the scent of the ingredients together gave him a shiver. Was he going to come right here? Apprehensively, he pulled the meat from the utensil with his teeth. The flavors cascaded over his tongue before he even began to chew. Ideas for cooking pork, onions, even apples fired off in his brain as though he had never tasted these things before and just now saw their potential. Another wave of pleasure rode through his body.

He was embarrassed, but the feeling was so small and distant compared to the building storm of flavors and ideas coursing through his brain that he couldn't concentrate on it. The room spun around him. His knees weakened. He stabbed at the next piece of pork, stuffing it into his mouth even as he dropped to the floor, completely overwhelmed by the experience.

When Simon returned to his senses, he was in the kitchen still, sitting in a chair on the other side of the island, feet in a trough of what looked like dirt which ran the length of the work surface. He tried to lift his right foot, but his muscles didn't want to respond. He tried the other to the same result.

"Chef?" Simon called, "Cecil?" There was no answer but the echo of his own voice off all the flat steel panels of coolers and the vent over the cook stations, the tile floors… Surely the chef wouldn't have left him, basically a stranger, in his kitchen alone. But no, they weren't strangers. Cecil had shared a recipe with him, inspired dozens of others, cooked for him, *just* him. The swinging doors opened. He looked up, expecting the chef.

No, this one was stout, square-faced, with slicked-back black hair, and not a nodule or protrusion out of the ordinary.

"Ah, you must be the new chef," the newcomer said, deeper than the chef's, and with a sinister edge.

"Where did Cecil go?" Simon demanded.

"*I'm* Cecil. I own this place. And now, I own *you*," the other said matter-of-factly as he walked around to the side. Simon looked up, mind reeling, trying to grasp what was happening.

"Own me? I'm an American citizen!"

"Of course you are, who else? Let's see how you're coming along." The man stepped closer and reached for the near flap of the white chef's jacket Simon just now realized he was wearing. He tried to turn away, then to hold the jacket closed with his hands, but the other was strong and he felt oddly weak, a bit floaty. Drugged?

Finally the cloth pulled to the side, revealing rows of tiny green leaves where his ribs had been, a nest of vines wrapped around his waist. A meaty, heavy, hand squeezed his pectoral muscles, his abs, then along his shoulders, his neck, his arms. "Yeah, you'll do. Not as big as the other guy was in the beginning, but you'll grow into the job, I'm sure."

"Job? I have a job, designing window displays and advertising materials for the mall."

"They won't miss you. This is a place you can really put down roots." The man laughed heartily, patting Simon on the back. "We open at six. Be ready."

"Be ready? I've never cooked for more than half a dozen…" The words faded out as visions of fry top and stove burners full of cooking food, of opening the oven and pulling out casseroles while others remained, not quite done. Knowledge flowed into him. Hundreds of recipes he'd never dared attempt now felt simple, passe. His feet tingled in the strange soil bath. Perhaps it was some kind of energizing practice, like a pre-game version of Epsom salts.

Grounding the word came to him and he laughed despite himself. Energy building, he felt strong enough to stand. He hauled himself up, but when he tried to step out of the trough, the soil resisted him. Packed too hard, maybe. He pulled again. The soil mounded up. His foot was caught on something. He yanked harder, shaking his leg.

Dirt fell away, revealing a tangle of white and tan roots. No. Wait. They looked like… No… No! He fell back, unable to lift his feet, crashing to the brown tile floor, sending the chair skidding away and falling with a clatter. His feet finally broke the surface of the dirt, revealing what had to be… Had to be the previous chef's twisted skeleton. The gold ring he had spotted earlier hung from one of the branched roots entangled around the ends of his legs.

He screamed, trying to pull away, but not even being able to get traction enough to drag himself from the trough. Something struck his belly. He looked down and the vines had grown small green tomatoes that swelled as he watched, beginning to redden.

The kitchen spun again.

Chef Simon slipped into oblivion.

Chef
de
Cuisine

Chef de Cuisine

Un conte délicieux raconté par

Mme Madi Quinn

"You mongrels!" Chef Carlo Giudice shouted, his face turning the familiar shade of purple. "This is unacceptable!"

Juliette, working hot apps this evening, was close enough to see Chef wind up to throw, but far away enough to have time to dodge. Others were not so lucky; Masako on salads received the full impact of the hurled beef flush on her cheek, knocking her off balance for a moment and nearly bringing her to tears. The chef did not care in which direction he lobbed an offending dish when he was displeased. No one was safe in his kitchen when someone dared bring him less than perfection.

Still, Chef Carlo Giudice was considered one of the top five chefs in the world. He was also known to be incredibly difficult to work for, thus if you could succeed under him, you were considered a good risk for your own restaurant, and investors tended to flock to you. That was Juliette's plan, anyway, though she had yet to rise to the rank of sous-chef, much less draw the attention of investors. It had been part of her elaborate plan since culinary school, one that she celebrated the advancement of once Chef Giudice had hired her to work for him at his flagship restaurant.

"Wilson!" the voice of the angered chef shattered Juliette's reverie. "Where is the goddamn capellini?"

Juliette looked down at the pan she was cooking and saw that the lobster capellini was ready. She took a quick taste to ensure that the pasta, the lobster, and the sauce seasoning were exactly the way they were supposed to be. "Walking capellini, chef!" Juliette proclaimed as she took the pan up for Chef's inspection.

Chef Giudice seized the pan from Juliette's hands as she approached, greeting her with an impatient scowl, and with a clean fork, tasted a bit of the dish for himself. The man himself was an intimidating figure, his head shaven and his beard close-cropped around his chin, trimmed to a point, resembling a sort of armor. Thin gray eyebrows framed ice-blue eyes that seemed to immobilize anyone on whom their gaze fell. He chewed a bit, then with a gruff nod, he dismissed her.

Relieved, Juliette returned to her station to cook the crab risotto on the next ticket. She put everything she had into every dish, and very rarely did she receive anything but the nod from Chef. It was the closest thing to praise anyone ever got. Never did he say "delicious" or "well cooked." Never. The nod was all you got unless he detonated on you.

Laurence, the fool working meat, brought up his hastily refired Wellington, praying that it was a perfect medium rare. Chances were good that if it wasn't, he would be fired. Chef was *that* exacting, and *that* volatile. This time, however, he was in luck, for he had the temperature correct, and he got a nod. Chef raised his finger in warning. It was Chef's way of saying "This is the one you get." Laurence scuttled back to his station, hurrying to cook the five waiting ribeyes. Dinner service waited for no one, and neither did Chef Giudice.

Finally, after another grueling service, Juliette wasted no time cleaning up her station, and preparing what she could for the next day's service. Chef appreciated efficiency, so what could be done ahead of time, she tended to do. Still, she was exhausted to the point of dizziness, and just wanted to fall into bed. Slowly, she trudged towards the exit door, but was intercepted by Masako, who had been working salads earlier during service.

"Juli, Chef wants to speak with you," Masako said, a slight tremor in her voice.

Juliette's forehead crinkled a little, confused as to what Chef could possibly want after her nearly flawless performance. It was not wise, however, to keep him waiting, so she wearily made her way up into Chef's office as soon as she could.

She opened the door into a Spartan, humble affair of an office, with only Chef's awards decorating the walls, including his Michelin stars and his James Beard awards. Chef himself sat behind a small wood desk. His face was contorted into a perpetual scowl, but now that scowl seemed to be somewhat relaxed, as if he were only angry at a few people as opposed to all of humanity. He gestured for Juliette to sit in one of the chairs in front of the desk.

"Wilson," Chef said, "sit."

Juliette did as bid and sat quickly and without comment.

"Thank you for coming," Chef continued, "I know this is very last minute so I will be brief. Tomorrow you start shadowing Tomas and training as sous-chef. It's your time."

"Thank you, Chef," Juliette said, her face deadpan.

"That will be all," Chef said, dismissing her.

Juliette rose and nodded respectfully to Chef, and walked out of the office, closing the door behind her. A smile crossed her face, and she mouthed the word "Yes!" Then, she walked quietly down the stairs from Chef's office and departed the restaurant, a new vigor filling her as she made her way to her car. Her drive home was filled with a new excitement that she could not contain; she had finally made it to the upper echelon, where she could finally get noticed for her own skills. The dream of her own restaurant was coming ever closer.

Her burst of energy did not last, however, and by the time Juliette got home, she was ready to shrug off her clothes and drop into bed, dreaming of what her dream restaurant's menu would be. She had hope now, even with Carlo Giudice's temper tantrums and ridiculous standards. He would not break her, nor would he take away her dream. There was nothing she would not do to make this dream happen. Nothing.

The next day came, and the cooks all assembled for prep, as they did every day. As Juliette arrived,

Masako pulled her aside, a sly look on her face.

"Some of us are meeting up after service tonight," Masako said. "You should come. We're meeting at Simon's Pub, ten o' clock."

Juliette nodded and smiled. "I'd like that. I'll be there."

Masako smiled at Juliette. "Great. I'll see you then."

Service was bustling, and Juliette had to remain on her toes from the beginning to the very end. Tomas was Chef's right-hand man, and the first line of defense when it came to quality. There was one undercooked appetizer that nearly got sent out, a situation that would have been far worse had she and Tomas not caught it. Still, everything ran as smoothly as could be expected, with Laurence taken off meat and put on hot apps, Masako on meat, the new hire Gary on garnish doing surprisingly well, and Heather returning from maternity leave to take over on salads.

By the time Juliette got to the pub, Laurence was already halfway through a large mug of beer, and two upturned shot glasses stood before Masako. Juliette sat down between them and ordered a rum and cola. Masako looked at her and smiled, clearly well down the road to intoxication.

"You're pretty," Masako said.

Juliette blushed slightly; Masako's bisexuality was the worst kept secret in the restaurant. "So, what's the little get-together all about, hmm?"

"Ah, yes," Laurence said, "well, we all had a purpose for working for Chef Giudice, yes? And it wasn't because of his sparkling wit and winning personality."

"I just assumed it was because we all want the prestige of working for that cockstain," Masako said.

"Well, yes, to make names for ourselves in the culinary world, and you do that by working for, shall we say, men like him." Laurence continued. "The problem is nobody's moving upwards. Chef likes keeping people where they are. So, we need to do something drastic. Something that's going to shake things up in this kitchen."

The bartender handed Juliette her drink, and she slipped him a ten. She then turned back to Laurence, wariness starting to show on her face. "Something like what?"

Masako looked around, trying so hard to be inconspicuous, but failing miserably. "Maybe we should retire to another seat, some place a little quieter."

The three rose from their seats and made their way to an empty booth in the back. Masako plopped down next to Juliette and draped an arm over Juliette's shoulder. Laurence rolled his eyes.

Juliette looked more than a little annoyed at this point. "Alright, what's going on?"

Laurence leaned in closer to Juliette, a wicked smile on his face. "We're gonna kill Chef."

Juliette leaned back, away from Laurence. "You…you can't be serious."

Shaking his head furiously, Laurence spoke far more calmly than Juliette felt he should. "Very serious.

We kill Chef, Tomas becomes the new executive chef, then everything gets restructured the way Tomas wants it. You're almost guaranteed to become his sous-chef, at least, and we all get a fair shake. We can make this work, Juli."

"No," Juliette protested. "No way. I'm already up for sous-chef training as it is, and I've got nothing to lose by letting things stay the way they are."

"No?" Masako asked. "Then why is the rumor going around that you're getting trained for sous-chef because you're getting shipped off to another restaurant?"

Juliette turned to Masako, her eyes wide with disbelief. "What? This is the first I've heard about it."

Masako nodded. "I heard it from Heather, and you *know* what the rumor about Heather's baby is, don't you?"

"No," Juliette said, shaking her head slowly, "what rumor?"

Masako laughed, downing another tequila shot. "Well…it's just a rumor, mind, but rumor has it that Heather got pregnant by Tomas."

"No!" Juliette gasped in disbelief. She'd never heard any of this, but then again, she very rarely engaged in the so-called "tea parties" that Masako and Laurence enjoyed so much.

"It stands to reason," Masako continued," if Tomas is sleeping with Heather, then he might be inclined to share little tidbits of information that he happens to know, such as where some up-and-coming sous-chefs are going to be reassigned to."

Juliette stopped what she was doing for a moment and thought. To be promoted to sous-chef was exactly what she wanted, but to be moved to another restaurant would be devastating to her career plans. She would essentially be stuck within Giudice's restaurants for the rest of her career. To get noticed, to catch the eye of investors, she had to remain under the gaze of Giudice himself, or at the very least, remain at the flagship restaurant. Anything else was unacceptable, and she *was* prepared to do *anything* to accomplish her goals…

But to kill Giudice? Could she raise her hand against the man who had given her a chance in the industry? Of course, he was also the man who threw food at her arbitrarily, who referred to her as a mongrel, a bitch, and worse, a man who could never be satisfied…

The man who was going to destroy her career.

"All right," Juliette said, warily. "I'm in."

Masako and Laurence smiled, nodding to each other. Masako tightened her grip around Juliette and laughed. "I'm so happy you're with us. I could kiss you."

Juliette returned the smile. "I really wish you wouldn't."

Laurence leaned in closer to his co-conspirators. "So, how are we going to do this?"

"The best option," Masako chimed in, "is to get Chef into the meat locker after service and do it there. It's easy to drain off any blood and it'd be the easiest area to clean up after."

"Okay," said Juliette, "but what are we going to

do with the body?"

There was silence for a moment. No one wanted to consider such a macabre subject.

Masako finally spoke up, "We'll dump it in the lake."

"Not a good idea," Juliette said. "We'd have to weigh it down. I watch a lot of true crime shows, and eventually bodies float to the top. There's only three of us, and none of us are all that strong."

"Speak for yourself," Laurence chirped. "I do Zumba!"

"You think dancing is going to help you heft four hundred pounds of Chef and weights into the lake?" Juliette asked, her eyes narrowing.

Laurence remained silent for a moment, then leaned back slightly on his bar stool. "No."

Masako downed another shot of tequila and flagged down the bartender to order a couple more. "We need a better plan than this. Something that's going to make this bastard vanish, not just hide him for a little while."

Juliette considered for a moment, and then closed her eyes. "I have an idea, but you're not going to like it."

"What?" Masako asked.

"If we need to make Chef disappear, there's really only one way to do that. We make other people make him disappear."

Masako and Laurence sat silent for a moment, then, as realization struck them, a look of horror came over them as they comprehended what Juliette was saying.

"No!" whispered Masako. "There is no way in Hell we're cooking and serving Chef to fucking customers!"

"Think about it. It gets rid of eighty percent of the body, and no one will ever find it, because it ends up being flushed down the toilet as customer shit. What's left, we bury deep in the city dump. It's straight out of the Grand Guignol, but it makes sense. It works."

"That's fucking sick, Juli," Laurence harshly whispered, his face turning green. "Sick."

"I'm not the one that decided to kill him. That was you. I'm just trying to figure out how to get away with it. You know I'm right."

"Can't we just get someone else in on this?" Masako asked.

Laurence shook his head. "We can't trust Heather or Gary. Heather's too close to Tomas and Gary's too new."

"I told you," said Juliette, "I'm right."

Laurence and Masako sat in silence for a moment, but eventually, unwillingly, nodded their acquiescence. Juliette nodded back, without a smile.

"So," Masako asked, "when do we do this?"

"The best time is Friday after service," Juliette said. "Chef usually has a little brandy afterwards, so he'll be slightly tipsy and easier to distract."

Laurence chimed in. "I'm not ready to do this on Friday. Let's do this next Friday."

Masako nodded. "I'd have to agree. This is a lot to work up to. Next Friday is better."

"Next Friday it is, then," Juliette said. "The asshole goes down."

Thus, it was that the fated day came, and the conspirators assembled for service as planned. Dinner service went as usual; Giudice threw his normal number of tantrums. Juliette *et al* dodged what items they could and endured the impact of what they could not. Shortly after service concluded, Chef Giudice retired to his office for his traditional nightcap. Tomas, on the other hand, seemed to want to linger, making the conspirators very nervous.

The three schemers kept to the shadows as they monitored Tomas waiting in the empty restaurant. He sat at one of the tables near the front door, as if he were waiting for someone. Sure enough, after a few minutes, Heather walked in from the break room where she'd been sitting, waiting for the right time to emerge. She sat down at the table next to Tomas, a look of desperation in her eyes.

"Please, Tomas, I need help," Heather pleaded. "I can't take care of a baby all by myself."

"And I already told you, I cannot afford to have my wife find out that I got someone pregnant," Tomas spat. "The consequences would be severe."

"More severe than being forced to raise your boss' child alone?"

"When this restaurant is mine, I can do more. Until then, I'm sorry, my hands are tied."

Heather glared at him with abject rage in her eyes. "You're a real bastard, Tomas. Sometimes I really hate what you've made me become."

Tomas hung his head. "Just a little time, Heather. You know I love you, but I can't survive her divorcing me. I'd be wiped out, and then *you'd* be supporting *me*."

"Fuck you, Tomas."

Heather stormed out of the dining room, and the sound of the back door slamming shut followed shortly thereafter. Tomas rose and followed after her, the door slamming shut a second time.

Masako looked to Juliette, her eyebrow raised slightly. "Interesting."

Juliette, Masako, and Laurence waited until they were sure that all other employees had left the restaurant, and then, summoning their courage, walked up the stairwell to the office of the chef.

Juliette knocked on the door and was immediately greeted with an annoyed bellow from within. "Who is it?"

"It's Juliette Wilson, Chef."

"Oh. Come in, Wilson."

Juliette entered the office as Masako and Laurence waited outside the office silently, waiting for the chef to pass through the doorway. Chef Giudice sat behind his desk, a small tumbler of brandy sitting on the desk and a very irritated expression on his face. "What is it, Wilson?"

"There's a problem in meat storage that you need to see, Chef."

"Have Tomas look at it."

"Tomas has left already."

"Son of a bitch!" Chef Giudice shouted, slamming his fist down on the desk. "I pay him enough, he should stick around longer than the goddamn *chefs de partie*. Can it wait until tomorrow?"

"I'm worried that we'll lose our entire stock of filets if we don't do something about it quickly, Chef."

Chef Giudice rolled his eyes. "Fine. Show me."

He slowly, warily, rose from behind the desk. He seemed suspicious, but that was nothing new; he was always suspicious of *something*. They reached the office door without incident, and Juliette took a moment to think to herself that just a few more steps and the plan was going to go into action…

They passed through the door, and Chef Giudice turned to his left and looked Masako right in the eye. "What the hell is this, Wilson? What's going o…"

He was unable to finish his sentence, as Laurence brought a nightstick down on the base of his skull, knocking him unconscious. Chef Giudice slumped to the landing in a heap.

Juliette sighed with relief. The first part of the

plan had been completed. Now for the hard parts. She grabbed Chef's hands and directed Laurence to grab his feet, and together they dragged the unconscious Chef down the stairwell and into the meat storage locker, making sure no one was there the whole way, and mostly closing the metal door behind them as to muffle any noise that might happen to come next. Using cooking twine, they tied Chef's hands and feet and propped him up against the back wall of the meat locker.

Juliette pulled a large chef's knife from a nearby block and leveled it at the heart of the unconscious chef but something was keeping her from going through with it. Was she having some doubts? Was there a chance in hell of them getting away with it? Questions began to fly through her head at the speed of light and she found herself confused. A pang of intense guilt surged through her as she tried to force herself to commit an act that she should find unspeakable, that society said was unspeakable, and yet, seemed to be little more to her than an obstacle in her path. Obstacles should be eliminated, and yet…there were still the faces of her parents, looking at her with disappointment. *Once again, you fail to stay in the lines, Juliette*, they seemed to say to her. Her brain felt as if it were on fire with conflict.

"I…I can't do it," Juliette said.

"I knew you couldn't finish the job," groaned Chef Giudice. "You're pathetic, all of you."

"Shut the hell up, old man!" shouted Juliette, the knife still pointed directly at the chef's heart.

"Or what?" Chef Giudice asked, spite dripping from his voice. "You already said you can't do it, so what do I have to worry about, you tickling me to death?"

"Do it!" screamed Masako. "Do it now!"

"Yes, Wilson, do it now, or I assure you, you will never work in a kitchen again. Soup kitchens will blacklist your miserable ass. Fast food places won't hire you. You've got no choice, Wilson. You have to either kill me or kill your pathetic career. Make your choice, Wilson. Make it now!"

Suddenly, Giudice's left leg lashed out hard, kicking the knife out of Juliette's hand. It fell to the ground, but as it did, Juliette went for the backup plan: a .45 caliber handgun she had stowed in her purse in case things went sour. Giudice was struggling and would likely work himself free within minutes if something wasn't done. She thrust the gun into his face without a thought.

"Shut up!" Juliette screamed, her body tensing and her finger squeezing the trigger.

The gun fired, one .45 caliber bullet going straight into Chef Giudice's face, blowing a hole in it the size of a ping pong ball, and blowing the entire back of his head out, splattering blood and brain all over the wall behind where his body leaned. The sound of the shot echoed loudly throughout the meat locker like an atomic bomb exploding in the faces of those who had gathered for murder, the remains of his head dripping slowly down the back wall of the locker. The three conspirators stood in stunned silence, staring at the bloodied corpse, scarcely able to believe that the fatal blow had been struck.

"The fuck, Juli?" Masako shrieked, after several moments of silence.

"I...I didn't mean to," Juliette whispered, her whole body trembling with something utterly unexpected: elation. "I tensed up and accidentally pulled the trigger."

"So what?" Laurence said, sounding relieved. "This was the plan, yes? It just went ahead a little early, and a little messier than we thought it would. Big deal. We stick to the plan."

The others nodded slowly, knowing exactly what that meant; they now had to not only cut up the body, but butcher him for use in the next dinner service. They had to make him into steaks, filets, and even some of his organs would find their way onto the menu.

Laurence went into another room off the main one and brought out thick plastic aprons and gloves. They all took a moment to silently tie the aprons on, without making eye contact, and then Juliette excused herself to fetch the knives and cleavers while Masako and Laurence lifted the body onto the butcher block.

Through the night, the three *chefs de partie* chopped, carved, and sliced the corpse into neat steaks and portions, placing the human meat in with the beef, pork, and lamb already within the restaurant. So precise was their work that the filet mignon of beef was barely distinguishable from the filet of chef. Had Chef Giudice been alive to see their work, he might have actually offered a word of praise, had it not been his flesh they were preparing, of course.

Dripping and drenched with blood and other ichors, the three chefs finally collected up what little remained of the erstwhile chef into an opaque plastic sack used for offal disposal. They then hosed down the meat locker to a sparkling shine, making certain no trace remained of the doomed chef, and shoved a pile of crates in front of the small hole where the bullet had impacted the back wall.

Perfection. No one would be the wiser, and

Carlo Giudice would have vanished from the face of the Earth. No longer would he torment anyone. In truth, he would do nothing ever again, except the one thing he never failed to do well; feed his hungry guests.

Without words, without looking at one another, the three chefs lugged the plastic sack with the last remnants of Chef Giudice out to Laurence's car and loaded it into the trunk. With any luck, he'd be able to get it out to the dump before daybreak, and dispose of it before anyone was the wiser. Everything seemed to be going exactly according to plan. Juliette found herself strangely pleased by this, as if she'd gambled with Fate itself, and won.

The next night's dinner service came, and the restaurant ran as usual, though the strange absence of Chef Giudice could not be explained. Tomas did a fine job taking control of the kitchen in Chef's absence, and service was completed with no major incidents. In truth, it seemed to go smoother than it usually did, with no outbursts of Chef's wrath causing delays.

The guests had nothing but positive things to say about the dishes that evening, wondering if somehow they'd gotten some better-quality meats, because there was a much different flavor, especially with the New York strip and the filet, and they seemed to prefer it to the usual prime or Wagyu beef. Juliette, working meats for the evening by Tomas' request, just smiled and turned out perfectly mid-rare steaks and chops, occasionally taking the chance to shoot a knowing nod to Masako or Laurence.

Chef had always claimed to put a little of himself into his dishes; this was merely the logical end to which he strove.

Service concluded, and the three conspirators smiled and went their separate ways without words, trying not to arouse any suspicion, but in their hearts they knew that they had gotten away with it. In fact, in a way, they had done the restaurant a favor.

Juliette's phone rang just as she arrived home. The display announced that it was Tomas. Her eyes went wide for a moment, and she swallowed hard. Had he discovered their crime? Was he calling the police to report their atrocity? She took a second to compose herself and answered the call. "Hello?"

"Juliette?" Tomas responded in his usual thick Spanish accent.

"Yes sir," Juliette said. "What can I do for you, Tomas?"

"I wanted to talk to you about tonight's service. Did you...do anything unusual to the meats?"

Juliette broke into a cold sweat. "What do you mean?"

"Our guests have been raving online about how exceptional the meats were. I wanted to tell you that whatever you did, keep doing it."

Unbeknownst to her, the guests had submitted reviews of the restaurant to various websites and apps stating that the meats at their restaurant were not only perfectly cooked, but also had incredible flavor unlike any other fine dining restaurant they'd ever patronized. Word of this got back to Tomas, which he took with great pride, but also to the investors of the restaurant, who began to question whether or not Giudice was the answer when after one night the average rating of the restaurant increased by one- and one-half stars.

Juliette breathed a silent sigh of relief. They remained undiscovered. "Of course, Tom…I mean, Chef."

"I like that. I think we're going to work well together. Good night, Juliette."

"Good night, Chef."

Juliette hung up and closed her eyes. There was such a thing as things working too well, and their plan had just done so. If all of a sudden the flavor of the meats went back to normal, the customers would inevitably complain, and that would prove almost as disastrous as if their crime were discovered. What good would getting away with murder be if her future plans were dashed? No, unfortunately what was needed was more of the proteins that the customers craved.

Which meant that more people had to die.

Why didn't that bother her? Moreover, why didn't the fact that she didn't know why bother her? Her parents had chided her constantly about her coloring books as a child, and her inability to stay in the lines. *You have to stay in the lines or it's wrong, Juliette*, they always said. *In coloring and in life*, they would say. This was far outside of the lines, and yet she felt… nothing. No guilt, no shame, no remorse. And no desire to stop. No, more people were going to have to die.

Not just any people, Juliette reasoned, because they had to be of similar physique to the late Chef. He was that perfect combination of fat and lean that lent itself to wonderfully marbled meats. Of course, she knew of one person that was just perfect, and would take care of one potential loose end as well.

Laurence.

She would have to be cautious though, for if everyone in the restaurant started disappearing, someone would inevitably get suspicious. No, he would be the last from the restaurant, but he was too perfect to let go. How to hunt him though…that would require some doing. She needed to clear her head, and to best do that, she needed to get her mind off of murder for a while. Remembering how Masako had ham-handedly flirted with her the night they had formed their conspiracy, Juliette shrugged and grinned. What could it hurt to spend a little time with the woman?

Juliette dialed Masako's number, and the slurring voice of the younger chef answered within a couple of rings. "'ello?"

"Masako?" Juliette said, her voice dripping with naughty intent.

"Is this Juliette?" Masako asked. "If it is, why don't you come over to my place? Then I won't be so… pathetic…by drinking alone."

"It *is* Juliette, and I'll be right over."

She hung up and, a wicked grin on her face, she made her way back out to the car, and back out onto the streets, headed for Masako's home.

She was greeted at the door by the reek of liquor being the only thing covering up the rank stench of vomit. Masako was clearly drunk; not just drunk, mind, but blind, stupid drunk. She was still able to recognize Juliette, however, and hugged her tightly.

"I di'n't think you were comin'," Masako slurred.

Juliette, in that moment, was filled with sinister purpose, a kind that she'd never felt before. Though she would definitely have to hunt Laurence, she could pump Masako for information, and then once that well ran dry, Masako would just be another loose end, an alcoholic one at that. If Juliette were to deal with her tonight, there would be one less mouth that could incriminate her, and one more night of wonderfully cooked meats to keep things going at the restaurant.

Juliette pulled herself close to Masako, her voice dropping to a sensual whisper. "Play your cards right and we *both* can."

Masako, somewhat shorter than Juliette, looked up into her eyes, confused. Then, realization washed over her like an unrelenting tide, and her face brightened into an excited smile as she leaned in closer, her eyes closing, and her lips trembling with expectation. Juliette leaned in to meet her, kissing her softly at first, then allowing the fever tide of passion to build. Masako wrapped her arms around Juliette's waist, holding her close, and letting her run her hands along Juliette's back.

Juliette discovered she was impatient, and quickly tore off Masako's top, causing the younger woman to reciprocate, pulling Juliette's sweater off and casting it aside. Masako grabbed Juliette by the hand and led her into her bedroom, which was a simple affair, a queen-sized bed with far too many plushies on it. Masako escorted Juliette to the bed as if she were royalty and bade her sit on the edge of the bed. Masako then stripped off what clothing she still had on, and stood naked before Juliette, as if trying to get her approval before continuing.

Juliette smiled, for Masako was not an unattractive woman, even though Juliette was not really into women. To be fair, Juliette had not had much in the way of emotional attachments to men either. She had her career, and that was all she needed. In addition, she'd known Masako had a crush on her for some time; it, like Masako's bisexuality, was one of the worst-kept secrets in the restaurant. There just had never been a reason to encourage her feelings until now, and although Juliette knew she wasn't looking for a relationship, they could at least say that they'd be together for the rest of Masako's life.

Now there were a few good reasons to encourage Masako, not the least of which was to entertain herself. What harm could come in some fun before the work had to be done?

Masako returned Juliette's smile, and approached slowly, kissing and caressing Juliette's face and neck. She then knelt down and slowly began to undress Juliette, first removing her jeans. Juliette enjoyed this sort of treatment and enjoyed having Masako provide it. Masako would shower each part of newly exposed skin with kisses, nibbles, and licks before she'd move on to the next garment, but soon enough, Juliette was as nude as Masako was, and Masako bade her lay down on the comfortable bed.

Masako began to nibble in Juliette's most sensitive places, generating in the woman a genuine arousal like she'd never known. Juliette had to give it to Masako: Masako was incredible in bed, though not enough to dissuade Juliette from her plan. There had been more foreplay in this encounter than in the last five years combined, and the irony made Juliette giggle. Masako didn't notice; she had a mouthful of nipple and wasn't concerned with a sudden outburst of happiness.

Masako used everything at her disposal to please Juliette; tongue, teeth, nails, even her breath was used to great effect in the right places. It wasn't long before Juliette had an incredible orgasm, driven there o the end of Masako's tongue. They held each other close after that, watched over by a mountain of plushies, and fell asleep in each other's arms.

Juliette woke after an hour or so and untangled herself from Masako's love grip. There was business to be done, and if it could be done while Masako was passed out drunk, so much the better. Juliette gathered her clothing together but didn't get dressed right away. There were things that she needed to be sure of first.

"Masako!" she whispered, louder than a normal whisper. "Masako!"

Masako did not stir, nor did she even so much as move. Juliette felt a pang of guilt well up in her gut as she looked down at Masako laying on the bed, naked, vulnerable, dreaming of the previous night. It wasn't too late, of course, and Juliette could do right by poor Masako, or at the very least just disappear out the door. Either would be better than what she had planned, but business was business, and nothing could be allowed to get in the way of Juliette's future.

Could she do it? Could she really murder someone she'd just slept with? She was barely able to kill Chef, and *that* was mostly accidental. She looked down once more at Masako asleep and closed her eyes. There was no choice. She had to.

Juliette quietly took hold of the pillow she had only minutes before been asleep on, and clutched it close to her body, waiting to see if Masako moved or made any sound. Part of her silently prayed that Masako would awaken before she could carry out such an obscene act and interrupt her. No movement, no sound came at all; only the silent movement of Masako's breathing as she slept the sleep of the drunken blissful. Then, as quietly as she had taken hold of the pillow, she forced it down on top of Masako's head with all her weight and force.

At first, there was no response, but as Masako began to suffocate, she began to thrash for her life, trying desperately to escape the unknown danger that threatened her. Juliette climbed on top of Masako's chest, straddling the smaller woman, and pinning her down, forcing the pillow down even harder, until eventually Masako stopped moving altogether.

Juliette continued to hold the pillow in place for several more minutes after Masako stopped moving, to ensure that she was actually dead. When she finally removed the pillow from Masako's still form, it was as if Masako's face was preserved forever in a ghastly masque of fear, her lips as blue as sapphire and her eyes ruby red from the burst blood vessels within. Masako had an unearthly beauty in death, and Juliette found herself leaning down to kiss those sapphire lips one final time before she had to take the body and dismember it for consumption.

She would have to do it alone; she couldn't have Laurence know that she'd killed Masako, or he'd know he was next. She also felt that after the intimacy that she and Masako had shared, it was only right that she butcher Masako herself. Masako was hers alone, and had been committed to her for the rest of her life, and Juliette felt this connection. No one else could be allowed to lay a hand on Masako.

Juliette got dressed and also put clothes on Masako's corpse, and lugged the body out the front door, as if helping a blacked-out drunk into a taxi. Enough of Masako's neighbors surely knew of Masako's habits; seeing her passed out would not be suspicious. Juliette "helped" Masako into her car, into the front seat, and buckled her in, all as if she were perfectly alive.

She went straight to the restaurant from there and dragged the inert form of Masako through the restaurant into the meat locker. She laid Masako across the butcher block gently, and carefully undressed her, making sure to cautiously pack away everything that would need to be destroyed as soon as she was done with her prep work. One final kiss on Masako's dead lips, and she used a cleaver to sever her head from her body.

The cooling blood trickled slowly from the wound. Juliette moved the body around to drain as much of it as possible. Next came the limbs, which were severed with care, not wanting to damage the tender meat that one could get around the shoulders and the thighs. Though Masako was in far better shape than Chef Giudice had been, she still could have stood to lose a pound or two, which made for premium cuts.

Juliette went to work with the more precise knives after that, separating specific muscle groups and particular bones, breaking down Masako's torso with skill. After about three hours, little remained of Masako beyond a head, some fingers, and a pile of organs that weren't usable. Juliette had decided to take Masako's heart for herself, as the heart was a much-sought-after meat, and she also wouldn't feel right if someone else had it. A half hour of cleanup in the meat locker, a few items stuffed in an offal bag, and once more no one would be the wiser.

Juliette returned home that night, a certain malaise having overcome her. It was the first time since this whole thing had begun that she wished she hadn't done what she'd done, but it was already over and couldn't be undone. Part of her felt her betrayal of Masako keenly, but the majority of her mind knew that she had to tie up all the loose ends if her plan was to come to fruition. The restaurant industry was extremely cutthroat; she just kicked it up a notch. She would have her own restaurant, no matter the cost. Juliette placed the container with Masako's heart in her freezer, and prepared for bed, hoping that service the next day would go more smoothly.

Dinner service came, and with the remnants of Chef Giudice to add to Masako's tender portions, Juliette was able to satisfy the throng that came because of the reviews they read online. Through the entirety of service, she kept one eye on Laurence, who seemed to be working as if nothing was wrong, fully convinced that he'd gotten away with murder.

As service concluded that night, Juliette invited the dwindling staff out to a night at Simon's Pub, to blow off some steam after the shocking disappearance of Chef Giudice, and now Masako's failure to show up for work. Most of the staff, including the wait staff, were keen to join her, as everyone had been affected by the changes going on in the restaurant, and everyone felt that a night out was a fine idea.

When Juliette arrived at Simon's, several people from the restaurant had already gotten there, including Laurence, Heather, Erik the maître d', Jillian and Mira from the front of house, and even Tomas had joined them. It was an impressive gathering of the team, and Juliette felt rather proud of herself. She did, however, have an ulterior motive; she was scouting out potential victims. Laurence for sure, but Jillian also looked like she might be suitable for serving to hungry guests.

Tomas was raving about how the critics were heaping the praise on the restaurant. So much so, in fact, that a national magazine was wanting to send a reporter to interview the head chef and get a feel for the scrappy restaurant that bounced back in the face of tragedy and went above and beyond where they'd been before. There was even talk of a famous television chef featuring it on one of his shows.

Juliette was distraught at this news; the last thing she needed was to have someone who's paid to dig up dirt digging around her restaurant. It could become messy, more so than what she'd already done.

No, she thought to herself, *we stick to the plan. The restaurant, the career is all that matters. Everything else is secondary.*

Laurence sat in one corner of the pub, looking particularly sullen, sipping slowly from his mug of beer. Juliette slid into the seat across the table from him and smiled her best smile.

"What's going on, man?" Juliette asked.

Laurence looked around the room, and then sighed. "You feel any regrets at all over…it?"

"Of course," Juliette lied. "I'm not a monster." Her ability to lie seemed to come naturally, as if she'd been doing it all her life.

Laurence sighed again. "It's hard, you know, living with this when you're alone. You go home and all you have are your thoughts."

"I agree," Juliette replied. "It is tough living alone with this kind of secret. I hear you there."

"So," Laurence continued, "why be alone?"

Juliette grinned at the ham-handed attempt at flirtation. She knew she had him, but to sink the hook in, she had to string him along a little first. "Laurence, are you flirting with me?"

"I might be."

"Well, don't take this the wrong way, hun, but I thought you were gay."

Laurence's eyes opened wide. "What? Of course not! Why would you think that?"

"You're a grown man that does Zumba and raises Corgis," Juliette wryly replied. "Do the math."

Laurence sighed once again, only this time there was a definite air of defeat in the sigh. "I'm not gay. In actuality, I'm quite interested in you."

Juliette grinned again. She had him now. "That's very sweet, but I don't really date co-workers."

What smile Laurence had on his face vanished, replaced by the sullen look he'd had prior to Juliette's arrival. "Oh. Of course, that's a wise idea."

"But that doesn't mean we can't be good friends, right?" Juliette continued, continuing to drive the fishhook deeper. "I mean, we carry this thing around, we need to support each other, right?"

"Yeah," Laurence wearily replied. "You're right, of course."

"Thank you, Laurence," Juliette said with a sly smile. "I'm glad I can count on you to be a good friend in this difficult time."

"You're welcome," Laurence replied, half of it said into the beer mug.

Juliette rose from the table and began to scan the room. Laurence would have to wait his turn. It would have to be someone from outside the restaurant this time, because there were questions being asked as it was, and if another person from the restaurant were to vanish without a trace, even more questions would be asked, and the police may even be involved. She could not have that. No, this time had to be an outsider, someone that wouldn't be immediately missed, especially at the restaurant.

Though the vast majority of people in the pub were employees of the restaurant, there were a few that were not, and Juliette focused her attention on them. One in particular caught her attention; a younger man, probably in his late twenties, that seemed the right build. He wasn't unattractive, *per se*, just a little out of shape and a little too fixated on his telephone to have much else going on. It made him an ideal target; flattery would get Juliette everywhere.

Juliette approached the table where the young man sat. He looked up from his phone as she approached, his eyes as big as saucers. The poor fool had no idea what he was up against, for even though Juliette was not supermodel-level attractive, and still looking a little disheveled from work, she knew what easy marks wanted, and she was capable of providing the promise of it.

"May I join you?" Juliette asked, her voice dripping with carnal promise.

"Umm…sure," the young man replied, his voice failing to produce much more than a tormented squeak.

Juliette slid into a chair across from the young man, her smile almost crocodilian, her ice-blue eyes never once taken off of her prey. She took the final sip from her drink as she did so, leaving only the last vestige of an ice cube in the glass. She closed her eyes slowly, and then reopened them with her gaze focused on the young man.

"Hi," she said, "I'm Juliette."

"Uhh, hey," the young man managed to fumble out, "George."

"Nice to meet you, George. What are you up to tonight?"

George fumbled with his phone for a moment, and then set the device down on the table. "Business stuff. Boring."

"Ah," Juliette replied, "What sort of business are you in?"

George chuckled. "Art sales. I basically hunt down pieces for rich people and acquire them by any means necessary."

"Sounds exciting."

George shrugged. "It can be, I suppose. Not everyone wants to let go of the pieces I'm to acquire. I do a lot of traveling, so that's nice. Kind of the Indiana Jones of the art world, in a way."

Juliette smiled. "Sounds way more exciting than what I do. I'm just a mere chef."

"Oh? Where do you work?"

"You're familiar with Carlo Giudice?"

George scoffed. "Who isn't?"

"I'm a sous-chef at his flagship restaurant."

George's expression went from interested to impressed. "That's hardly a 'mere' anything. I hear Giudice is a real ballbuster."

Not anymore, Juliette thought. "Yeah, he's a taskmaster, but he makes you push yourself to be the best you can be. I don't see a thing wrong with that."

"I don't suppose you can get me a reservation," George laughed.

Gotcha, Juliette thought. "I can do better than that. I can give you a personal tour of the restaurant."

"I'm listening."

Juliette rose from her seat and casually walked around the table to whisper in George's ear. "Do you wanna fuck in the restaurant?"

George swallowed his mouthful of drink. "Very much."

"Let's go."

Juliette took George by the hand. Juliette could not help but notice the gleam of jealousy and wrath in Laurence's eye as she led the mark out of the pub to his room. That was good; it was exploitable for next time. In the meantime, George was eating out of her hand, and would do whatever she asked, so long as he thought there was pussy at the end of the rainbow.

At the restaurant, she fumbled with the keys, anticipation starting to get the better of her. She punched Tomas' alarm code in, the one she'd seen him enter in a hundred times, and they entered the darkened restaurant.

George looked around the back of the house, starstruck. "Wow. You really do work here! For a moment I thought you were just making shit up to get in my pants."

Juliette laughed, though she envisioned sticking a finger down her throat. "No, I really do work here. And…let's be honest, George…I don't have to make shit up, do I?" She pressed herself up against George, running a hand down his chest.

"No, not really."

Juliette moved in and softly kissed George, leaving the young man speechless. "Do you want to fuck in Giudice's office? Even *he* doesn't do that."

"Yes," George squeaked.

Juliette took George by the hand once more, leading him to the stairs in the back of the restaurant. Before they walked up the stairs, she kissed him, giving him a taste of things he was to think were coming. She was revolted by the young man's beer breath, but she had to repress every instinct, every emotion she had. She had to make the act convincing. She couldn't be herself with this stranger; she had to be the perfect slut, the dream of every post-adolescent straight man. The woman that wanted nothing but to bang. It offended her in a thousand different ways, but it was how she was going to trap her prey.

"Let's go upstairs, George."

They walked slowly up the stairs until they reached the landing before the office. Once more, Juliette kissed the young man, this time letting him paw at her with his clumsy hands. He didn't seem to know what he was doing at all, as if a woman's body was merely something for him to play with for his own gratification and nothing more. His age was the first clue, but his fumbling about clinched it; he was a virgin.

"A shame," Juliette whispered.

"What?"

Juliette lashed out hard with a swift kick to the kneecap followed by a hard shove, and George flew backwards with a look of utter shock on his face. He tumbled down the stairs head over heels and landed headfirst on the first floor with the sickening thud of his head smashing against the wall. Juliette quickly ran down the stairs after him and checked to see if he was still alive. He was still breathing. He had landed right on his head and neck which had seemed to put him out for a bit. This was inconvenient for Juliette, as she'd always had to butcher the meat from corpses. To butcher this one would involve restraint and keeping the noise to a minimum. More hassles. She sighed with resignation and dragged the man into the meat locker and set herself to prep work.

Three hours later, long after the screaming had come to an end,   Juliette set to cleaning up the mess that had been made as she had been doing prep work. George had bled quite a bit as she dragged him into the meat locker, so she had to mop up what had spilled outside of the locker while the hose inside washed away the remnants of his blood in the locker. It had been a messy kill, certainly more of a mess than Masako had been, but now it was done, and she could clean up and move on, preparing for the next one, which would inevitably be Laurence. In a way, she dreaded that kill more than this one, because there were stakes involved with Laurence that just didn't exist with George. Laurence was a friend, a co-worker, and a co-conspirator. Just as Masako hurt, Laurence would also hurt. That's how normal people, people who color inside the lines are supposed to feel when they murder someone.

The thing was, George didn't hurt at all. She had felt nothing but annoyance as the man had screamed, desperate for his life, as she hacked off limbs. Sure, watching your own body being dismantled was uncomfortable at best, but even as George struggled against the improvised restraints Juliette had fashioned from bungie cords and duct tape, she'd felt nothing but the need to get the work done. Even as he saw his own limbs piled in front of him, screaming for help that was not coming, she felt little to nothing.

She wasn't staying in the lines, and she didn't care.

Juliette thought back to Masako, and she found herself wishing that she felt something about it. The closest thing to a relationship she'd had for years was with Masako, and for that one beautiful night, that one pristine night, they'd savagely enjoyed each other. Juliette genuinely believed that she missed Masako, even though she knew Masako's heart was just waiting for her in her freezer. Would killing Laurence feel like this? Would ending his life make an empty place in her heart just as Masako had?

Would she need to take his heart too? It was getting crowded in that freezer.

Juliette sighed; she would worry about that when she had to worry about it. At that moment she needed to get George's blood off the floor before she could get some sleep. It was her day off, and she wanted nothing to do with cooking anything if she could get away with it. She would order bad take out if she got hungry and stay far away from the freezer.

Juliette's day off passed with little incident. She received a phone call from Laurence asking if she'd seen Masako, to which she lied convincingly enough by claiming that she hadn't seen Masako since the night they had dealt with Chef Giudice, and that if he wanted to find Masako, he should check her place. He'd likely find her passed out drunk there. It was believable enough for Laurence, as Masako's penchant for drinking was pretty well known, but it left Juliette with a heavy heart. She dismissed the feeling almost as quickly as it came on; she couldn't afford guilt at this point in the venture. Nothing, not even her own conscience, could be allowed to get in the way of her future.

Juliette thawed Masako's heart and made an excellent tartare with it, even though she wasn't expecting any company. It was logical; it was far easier to explain the presence of a steak tartare than it was to explain the presence of a human heart, especially the one of a missing woman. Not that she expected the police to show, but one had to be prepared for all contingencies when one crossed the line into murder and cannibalism.

The tartare truly was excellent. It had been a long time since she'd made one, since Giudice rarely changed his menu. Part of her hoped that Tomas wouldn't prove as inflexible because she needed to spread her wings as an artist. Food was art to Juliette, and even something as macabre as a human heart could be fashioned into something beautiful by a sufficiently talented chef, and Juliette felt herself sufficiently talented. After all, it was her skill with knives that was bringing the restaurant to a whole new level of success, was it not?

It certainly wasn't Laurence. He was a pretender, a culinary school graduate who thought he knew everything, but in truth he didn't understand the artistry of food. Oh, he could cook a steak, but he didn't understand plating at all. He didn't understand why you don't pre-slice a filet or why you don't just dump the mash anywhere on the plate for the beef Wellington. While it was true that not everyone would become a *chef de cuisine*, he had the balls to declare that one day he would be running his own restaurant. To Juliette, the very thought was an insult, but Masako had been friends with the lout, so she had tolerated him.

Masako was gone, and soon, he would be too.

Juliette went out that evening on the hunt, because even though she'd been off that day, she knew that Laurence, lazy as he was, would not restock the meats properly. She would have to do it, and there was only one way. She would have to hunt in another bar, because if patrons of Simon's started to vanish after leaving with her, the finger would be pointed right at her, and rightly so. No, she had to keep everything random, with no discernible pattern. She couldn't allow herself to be caught. Nothing could get in her way.

At a nondescript bar on the other side of town, she found another perfect mark; young, plump, and stupid. He was easy enough to manipulate, just as George had been. She lured him into her trap, and by the time he figured out anything was wrong, she had plunged a chef's knife in between his vertebrae. The young man fell to his knees first, and then fell forward with a loud thud onto the tiled floor of the meat locker. The black widow had struck again.

She'd gotten the butchery process down to a science by this point, so breaking the body down was only a two-hour act. Once they were dead, Juliette no longer saw them as human; they were simply another carcass to be butchered into so much meat, no more than a side of beef. She'd also become quite fastidious about maintaining a consistent size and thickness for each and every cut. She took pride in her work.

She cleaned up the mess, which was far less than there had been the previous night and locked up. Once she dumped the scraps, she would have a well-earned rest. She was back at work the next day, and that would also be the day that "dear" Laurence met his fate. If someone like Masako had to die, then he most assuredly would have to die as well. It was only a matter of time.

Morning came, and Juliette rose from her sleep, refreshed and ready. It was the day that she had awaited, the day she had planned for. Laurence's judgment day had come at last.

Juliette dined on a bit of the tartare she'd made and fresh, hot coffee. The cold meat and hot coffee filled her in a way that was hard to describe, an odd contrast that somehow worked, and she felt strong, powerful. She knew that she would have what was necessary to do what needed to be done.

She got in the shower and let the scalding water cascade over her. She didn't want to think about food or hunting or prep work for a little while; she just wanted some time to herself. Yet, she found herself almost longing for Masako to be there with her, in that steaming hot shower, their bodies pressed together. She had felt *something* in their short time together, and that something confused and terrified her. That something distracted her from her plan, and she could not have it.

And yet it was there, haunting her when she let her guard down.

She pushed it away, shoving all emotion into the back of her mind. It was time to go to work and prepare for the most important hunt yet. Through the whole drive to the restaurant, all she allowed herself to think about was how she was going to lure Laurence into the meat locker. Any thoughts of Masako were dismissed immediately.

Juliette found herself assigned to meats once again, and she set herself to work preparing her station, but one eye was always kept on Laurence. He seemed to suspect nothing, for he was going about his business as usual. She even shot him a sly smile, a smile that was returned by the future rack of "lamb". He seemed clueless, and that worked in her favor. He would prove easier to manipulate than she feared.

Juliette formulated a plan as she cooked throughout the night, because there was no choice. It had to happen that night. She would entice Laurence into the meat locker, and then kill him there, probably by cutting his throat. She would drain him of blood, and then butcher him, portion him, and that would be that. She was content with her plan and steeled herself and her will in preparation for carrying it out.

Finally, dinner service concluded, and everyone began to scatter. As Laurence began to head for his car, Juliette caught up to him, a wan look in her eye.

"Laurence, do you have a minute?" she asked.

"Sure," he responded. "What's up?"

"I…oh, God, this is hard. You know how I've said in the past I don't want to date co-workers?"

Laurence nodded. "Yeah, I recall being shot down by that logic."

A knot began to form in Juliette's stomach, though she wasn't sure if it was nerves or guilt. "I…uh…am changing that policy."

Laurence brightly smiled. "About goddamn time."

"How about you," Juliette said, grabbing Laurence by the edges of his jacket, "meet me in the meat locker in about twenty minutes, and we work on making up for lost time."

Laurence raised an eyebrow. "Odd choice for a rendezvous, but alright. Twenty minutes."

Juliette smiled at him, then turned and walked back into the restaurant, her smile vanishing as soon as she was out of sight. It was time for business.

She grabbed one of the large chef's knives from her knife set and felt its weight in her hand. Then, quietly as she could, she crept into the shadows of the restaurant now that everyone had already left and shut the majority of the lights off. Finally, the twenty minutes passed, and Laurence crept into the back entrance of the restaurant and made his way into the meat locker.

Juliette sneaked up behind him as soundlessly as she could, but a misstep gave away her presence, and Laurence spun around to see her with a large knife in her hand at the ready and he raised his hands in front of him in defense. Juliette swung the knife in a wide arc, slicing his hands, which forced him to recoil in pain. She slashed back in the opposite direction, missing him completely, and leaving herself open for him to lash out with a foot to her abdomen. She flew backwards, landing hard against the wall and letting go of the knife.

Laurence, seeing the knife fall to the ground, immediately dove for it, but Juliette drove her heel hard into his outstretched hand, crunching bone and causing him to howl in agony. Juliette snatched up the knife and slashed randomly in front of her, not really making

contact but driving Laurence back and away from her as she regained her footing. He also clambered to his feet and made a last-ditch effort to get the knife away from Juliette, lunging at her. Juliette managed to shift her arm just enough to intercept the lunge, and instead of hitting Juliette, he impaled himself on the knife by the throat.

Laurence fell to his knees, making sickening gurgling and choking sounds. Juliette placed one foot upon his chest and grabbed the hilt of the blade, and pushed off, shoving Laurence backwards and pulling the knife free of his throat. He fell to the ground and blood oozed from the wound, the gurgling and gasping becoming louder as he drowned in his own blood. It didn't take long before all was quiet and the *chef de partie* lay still, ready for preparation. Juliette slowly dragged the carcass up and onto the butcher block, and grabbed a cleaver, preparing for her macabre work.

The door to the meat locker opened. She looked up and saw Tomas, his arms folded and a scowl of rage on his face. He glared at her for several moments without saying a word.

Then he walked away silently, and the cleaver fell.

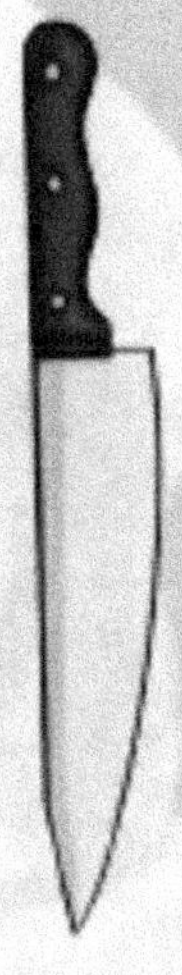

Closing Credits

Madi Quinn (featured author):

Who do you thank first when you have so many to thank? First I want to thank w.p. Quigley for his seemingly endless patience with a very slow learner; S N Humphreys, John A. McColley, and DS Vernon for their boundless diligence and care in all things editorial; Lucienne LeBeau for simply being the most awesomest; Sumiko Saulson (the Award-Winning Sumiko Saulson, I mean) for looking my book over when I really, desperately needed someone to do so; and of course to my stalwart partner Mary, for forgiving me those nights when I just HAD to get up and write at 3 A.M.

John A. McColley (issue editor, author - "Shift Change"):

Cindy, Ethan, Marilyn, Byron, Christine, Grady, and Kristin — who have kept me moving forward on all my creative projects through their support on Patreon, despite my use of Oxford Commas. The AP Family, as always.

w.p. Quigley (wanted felon, author — "Tootsie Roll"):

Cinemax after dark, the Spice Channel, internet porn, and yo mama.
For real though: Ascendent staff - past, present, and future, regardless of who you are.